"I've rearranged my schedules and jetted all over Europe for you. I'm doing my level best right now not to use sex as a weapon. What the hell else do yo

"I don't know!"

"When you figure it o a hard voice. Getting pockets. "Until then, I'm going to keep on walking away from you, even though it half-kills me every time."

"Me, too."

The quiver in her voice went right through him. "God, Clea, the last thing I want to do is fight with you after the night you've had. Get into bed and go to sleep."

In a flash of bare thighs she slipped under the puffy white duvet. "I'll see you in New York," she said.

Leaning over, he switched out the bedside lamp. The darkness giving her courage, Clea announced, "Until I met you, I was always the one calling the shots."

He laughed. "You know what? The same's true of me."

His eyes adjusting to the gloom, he strode toward the door of the suite. His whole body ached with frustration. He'd walk all the way to his hotel. Perhaps it would take his mind off sex. Off the beautiful redhead alone in her hotel room, where he'd left her.

The woman who was changing his life.

Although born in England, **Sandra Field** has lived most of her life in Canada; she says the silence and emptiness of the north speaks to her particularly. While she enjoys travelling, and passing on her sense of a new place, she often chooses to write about the city which is now her home. Sandra says, 'I write out of my experience; I have learned that love with its joys and its pains is all-important. I hope this knowledge enriches my writing, and touches a chord in you, the reader.'

Recent titles by the same author:

HIS ONE-NIGHT MISTRESS
THE ENGLISH ARISTOCRAT'S BRIDE

THE JET-SET SEDUCTION

BY
SANDRA FIELD

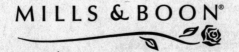

First published in Great Britain 2006
Harlequin Mills & Boon Limited,
Eton House, 18-24 Paradise Road, Richmond, Surrey TW9 1SR

© Sandra Field 2006

ISBN 0 263 84819 1

Set in Times Roman 10½ on 11½ pt.
01-0606-52080

Printed and bound in Spain
by Litografia Rosés, S.A., Barcelona

CHAPTER ONE

A GARDEN party. Not his usual scene.

Slade Carruthers had stationed himself in one corner of the garden, a palm tree waving high over his head, his back flanked by California holly. The sun was, of course, shining. Would it dare do anything else for Mrs. Henry Hayward III's annual garden party?

He was here on his own. As he preferred to be.

He was in between women right now; had been for quite a while. Maybe he'd grown bored with the age-old game of the chase, and the inevitable surrender that led, equally inevitably, to the end of yet another affair. Certainly for quite a while he hadn't met anyone who'd tempted him to abandon his solitary status.

Casually Slade looked around. Belle Hayward's guests were, as usual, an eccentric mixture of extremely rich, well-bred socialites and artistic mavericks. But every one of them knew the rules: suits and ties for the gentlemen, dresses and hats for the ladies. The two large men stationed at the iron gates had been rumored to turn away a famous painter in acrylic-spattered jeans, and an heiress in diamond-sprinkled capri pants.

The Ascot of San Francisco, Slade thought, amused. His

own summerweight suit was hand-tailored, his shoes Italian leather, his shirt and tie silk. He'd even combed his unruly dark hair into some sort of order.

A young woman strolled into his field of view. Her head was bent as she listened to an elderly lady who looked familiar to Slade, and who was wearing a mauve gown that looked all too recently resurrected from mothballs. He searched for her name, realizing he'd met her here last year. Maggie Yarrow, that was it. Last of a line of ruthless steel magnates, possessor of a tongue like a blunt ax.

The young woman had broken both Belle's rules. She was hatless and she was dressed in a flowing tunic over wide-legged pants.

Her wild tangle of red curls shone like flame in the sunlight.

Slade left his post under the palm tree and started walking toward her, smiling at acquaintances as he went, refusing a goblet of champagne from one of the white-jacketed waiters. His heart was beating rather faster than he liked.

As he got closer, he saw she had wide-spaced eyes of a true turquoise under elegantly arched brows; a soft, voluptuously curved mouth; a decided chin that added character to a face already imbued with passionate intelligence.

And with kindness, Slade thought. Not everyone would have chosen to pass the afternoon with a rude and dotty ninety-year-old. His nose twitched. Who did indeed smell of mothballs.

Then the young woman threw back her head and laughed, a delightful cascade of sound that pierced Slade to the core. Her hair rippled over her shoulders, gleaming as a bolt of silk gleams in the light.

He stopped dead in his tracks. His palms were damp, his heart was racketing in his chest and his groin had hardened. How could he be so strongly attracted to someone whose name he didn't even know?

It looked as though his long months of abstinence were over. If he didn't meet her, he'd die.

Where the hell had that thought come from? Cool it, he told himself. We're talking lust here. Plain old-fashioned lust.

As though she sensed the intensity of his gaze, the young woman looked straight at him. Her smile faded, replaced by a look of puzzlement. "Is something wrong?" she said. "Am I supposed to know you?"

Her voice was honey-smooth, layered like fine brandy; she had the trace of an accent. Slade said, "I don't believe we've met, no. Slade Carruthers. Hello, Mrs. Yarrow, you're looking well."

The elderly lady gave an uncouth cackle. "Watch out for this one, girl. Richer than you by a city mile. Money and machismo—he's one of Belle's favorites."

"Why don't you introduce me anyway?" Slade said.

"Introduce yourselves." Maggie Yarrow hitched at the shoulder of her gown. "Look at the pair of you—an ad for Beautiful People. California Chic. I need more champagne."

Slade ducked as she swished her ebony cane through the air to get the attention of the nearest waiter. After grabbing a glass from his tray, she tossed back its contents, took another from him and walked in a dead-straight line toward her hostess.

Trying not to laugh, Slade sought out those incredible turquoise eyes again. "I'm not from California. Are you?"

"No." She held out one hand. "Clea Chardin."

Her fingers were slender, yet her handclasp was imbued with confidence; Slade always paid attention to handshakes. It also, he thought shakily, carried a jolt like electricity. He opened his mouth to say something urbane, witty, erudite. Instead he heard himself say, "You're the most beautiful woman I've ever met."

Clea tugged her hand free, to her dismay feeling desire

uncoil in her belly; every nerve she possessed was suddenly on high alert. Danger, she thought. This man wasn't her usual fare. Far from it. Taking a deep breath, she said lightly, "I read an article recently that said beauty is based on symmetry. So you're complimenting me because my nose isn't crooked and I'm not wall-eyed."

Pull out all the stops, Slade thought. Because this is a woman you've got to have. "I'm saying your eyes are like the sea in summer when it washes over a shoal. That your hair glows like the coals of a bonfire on the beach."

Disconcerted, Clea blinked. "Well," she said, "poetry. You surprise me, Mr. Carruthers."

"Call me Slade...and I can't imagine I'm the first man to tell you how astonishingly beautiful you are." He smiled. "Actually, your nose is slightly crooked. Adds character."

"You mean I'm imperfect?" she said. "Now your face is much too strong to be called handsome. Compelling, yes. Rugged, certainly." She smiled back, a smile full of mockery. "Your hair is the color of polished mahogany, and your eyes are like the Mediterranean late on a summer evening—that wonderful midnight-blue."

"You're embarrassing me."

"I can't imagine I'm the first woman to tell you how astonishingly attractive you are," she riposted.

"You know what? Your skin's like the pearly sheen inside a seashell." And how he longed to stroke the hollow beneath her cheekbone, its smooth ivory warmth. Fighting to keep his hands at his sides, Slade added, "A mutual admiration society—is that what we are?"

"From the neck up only," Clea said, deciding the time had come for a solid dose of the truth. "I'm not going near your body."

He dropped his iron control long enough for his gaze to

rake her from head to toe, from her softly shadowed cleavage to the seductive flow of waist, hip and thigh. On her bare feet she was wearing jeweled sandals with impossibly high heels. My God, he thought, I'm done for. "That's very wise of you," he said thickly, and looked around the crowded garden. "Given the circumstances."

"I meant," she said clearly, "that I'm literally not going near your body."

"Scared to?"

"Yes."

His choke of laughter was involuntary. "You're honest, I'll say that for you."

She gave him an enigmatic smile; at least, she hoped it was enigmatic. "Where's home for you, Slade?"

Tacitly accepting her change of subject, he answered, "Manhattan. And you?"

"Milan."

"So your accent's Italian?" he said.

"Not really. I grew up in France and Spain."

"What brings you here?"

"I was invited."

An answer that wasn't an answer. He glanced down at her aqua silk trousers. "How did you get past the dragons at the gate? Belle's dress code is set in concrete."

She said demurely, "I arrived earlier in the day and changed in the house."

"So you know Belle well?"

"I'd never met her before yesterday…nor had I met Maggie Yarrow. Just how rich are you, Slade Carruthers?"

"I could ask the same of you."

"Carruthers…" Her eyes widened. "Not Carruthers Consolidated?"

"The same."

"You're doing all that cutting-edge research on environ-mentally sustainable power sources," she said with genuine excitement, temporarily forgetting that Slade represented nothing but danger. She asked a penetrating question, Slade answered and for ten minutes they talked animatedly about wind power and solar systems.

Although she was both informed and interested, it was he who brought the conversation back to the personal. "How long are you staying in the area? I could show you the project we're working on outside Los Angeles."

"Not long enough for that."

"I have a house in Florence," he said.

She smiled at him, her lips a sensual curve. "I spend very little time in Italy."

He couldn't invite her for dinner tonight; it was a yearly ritual that he have dinner with Belle after the garden party so she could dissect all the guests and savor the latest gossip. "Have dinner with me tomorrow night."

"I already have plans," she said.

"Are you married? Engaged?" Slade said, failing to dis-guise the urgency in his voice. He had a few inflexible rules as far as women were concerned, one being that he never had an affair with a woman who was already taken.

"No and no," she said emphatically.

"Divorced?" he hazarded.

"No!"

"Hate men?"

Clea smiled, her teeth even and white, her eyes laughing at him. His head reeled. "I like the company of men very much."

"Men in the plural."

She was now openly laughing. "In the plural overall, one at a time in the specific."

Didn't he operate the same way with women? So why did

he hate her lighthearted response? He said, "I'm not inviting you for dinner tonight because Belle and I have an annual and long-standing date."

Clea's lashes flickered. For her own reasons, she didn't like hearing that Slade Carruthers and Belle were longtime friends. She said calmly, "Then perhaps we aren't meant to talk further about windmills."

"Meet me tomorrow morning at Fisherman's Wharf," Slade said.

"Why would I do that?"

Because you're so beautiful I can't think straight. "So I can buy you a Popsicle."

"Popsicle?" She stumbled over the word. "What's that?"

"Fruit-flavored ice on a stick. Cheap date."

She raised her brows artlessly. "So you're tight with your money?"

"I don't think you'd be overly impressed were I to splash it around."

"How clever of you," she said slowly, not altogether pleased with his small insight into her character.

"Ten in the morning," he said. "Pier 39, near the Venetian carousel. No dress code."

"Beneath your charm—because I do find you charming, and extremely sexy—you're ruthless, aren't you?"

"It's hard to combine raspberry Popsicles with ruthlessness," he said. Sexy, he thought. Well.

"I—"

"Slade, how are you, buddy?"

Slade said, less than enthusiastically, "Hello there, Keith. Keith Rowe, from Manhattan, a business acquaintance of mine. This is Clea Chardin. From Milan. Where's Sophie?"

Keith waved his glass of champagne somewhat drunkenly in the air. "Haven't you heard? The Big D."

Clea frowned. "I don't understand."

"Divorce," Keith declaimed. "Lawyers. Marital assets. Alimony. In the last four months I've been royally screwed—marriage always boils down to money in the end, don't you agree?"

"I wouldn't know," Clea said coldly.

Slade glanced at her. She was pale, her eyes guarded. But she'd never divorced, or so she'd told him. He said, "I'm sorry to hear that, Keith."

"You're the smart one," Keith said. "He's never married, Chloe. Never even been engaged." He gulped the last of his champagne. "Evidence of a very shu—oops, sorry, Chloe, what I meant was superior IQ."

"Clea," she said, even more coldly.

He bowed unsteadily. "Pretty name. Pretty face. I've noticed before how Slade gets all the really sexy broads."

"No one gets me, Mr. Rowe," she snapped. "Slade, I should be going, it's been nice talking to you."

Slade fastened his fingers around the filmy fabric of her sleeve to stop her going anywhere. Then, in a voice any number of CEOs would have recognized, he said, "Keith, get lost."

Keith hiccuped. "I can take a hint," he said and wavered across the grass toward the nearest tray of champagne.

"He's a jerk when he's sober," Slade said tightly, letting go of Clea's sleeve, "and worse when he's been drinking. Can't say I blame Sophie for leaving him."

Heat from Slade's fingers had burned through her sleeve. Danger, her brain screamed again. "So you condone divorce?" Clea said, her voice like a whiplash.

"People make mistakes," he said reasonably. "Although it's not on my agenda. If I ever get married, I'll marry for life."

"Then I hope you enjoy being single."

"Are you a cynic, Clea?"

"A realist."

"Tell me why."

She gave him a lazy smile that, Slade noticed, didn't quite reach her eyes. "That's much too serious a topic for a garden party. I want one of those luscious little cakes I saw on the way in, and Earl Grey tea in a Spode cup."

Much too serious, Slade thought blankly. That's what's wrong. I'm in over my head, drowning in those delectable blue-green eyes. When have I ever wanted a woman as I want this one? "I'll get you whatever you desire," he said.

Her heart gave an uncomfortable lurch in her chest. "Desire is another very big topic. Let's stick to *want*. What I want is cake and tea."

Visited by the sudden irrational terror that she might vanish from his sight, he said, "You'll meet me tomorrow morning?"

He wasn't, Clea was sure, a man used to being turned down; in fact, he looked entirely capable of camping out on her hotel doorstep should she say no. Better, perhaps, that she meet him in a public place, use her usual tactics for getting rid of a man who didn't fit her criteria, and then go back to Belle's on her own.

"Popsicles and a carousel?" she said, raising her brows. "How could I not meet you?"

"Ten o'clock?"

"Fine."

The tension slid from his shoulders. "I'll look forward to it." Which was an understatement if ever there was one.

She said obliquely, "I leave for Europe the next day."

"I leave for Japan."

Her lashes flickered. "Maybe I'll sleep until noon tomorrow."

"Play it safe?" He grinned at her. "Or do I sound incredibly arrogant?"

"I only take calculated risks," she said.

"That's a contradiction in terms."

She said irritably, "How many women have told you your smile is pure dynamite?"

"How many men have wanted to warm their hands—or their hearts—in your hair?"

"I don't do hearts," Clea said.

"Nor do I. Always a good thing to have out in the open."

She looked very much as though she was regretting her decision to meet him, he thought. He'd better play it cool, or Clea Chardin would run clear across the garden path and out of his life.

"Tea and cake," he said, and watched her blink. Her lashes were deliciously long, her brows as tautly shaped as wings. Then she linked her arm with his; the contact surged through his body.

"Two cakes?" she said.

"A dozen, if that's what you want," he said unsteadily.

"Two is one too many. But sweets are my downfall."

"Clams and French fries are mine. The greasier the better."

"And really sexy broads."

He said flatly, "Let's set the record straight. First, I loathe the word *broad*. Secondly, sure I date. But I'm no playboy and I dislike promiscuity in either sex."

So her tactics were almost sure to work, Clea thought in a flood of relief. "This is a charming garden, isn't it?" she said.

For the first time since he'd seen her, Slade looked around. Big tubs of scented roses were in full bloom around the marquee, where an orchestra was sawing away at Vivaldi. The canopy of California oaks and palm trees cast swaying patterns of shade over the deep green grass, now trampled by many footsteps. The women in their bright dresses were like flowers, he thought fancifully.

Because Belle's garden was perched on one of the city's hilltops, a breeze was playing with Clea's tangled curls. He reached over and tucked a strand behind her ear. "Charming indeed," he said.

Her eyes darkened. Deliberately she moved a few inches away from him, dropping her hand from his sleeve. "Do you see much of Belle?" she asked.

"Not a great deal. I travel a lot with my job, and my base is on the East Coast…how did you meet her?"

"Through a mutual friend," Clea said vaguely; no one other than Belle knew why she was here. "Oh look, miniature éclairs—do you think I can eat one without getting whipped cream on my chin?"

"Another calculated risk," he said.

"One I shall take."

Had he ever seen anything sexier than Clea Chardin, in broad daylight and surrounded by people, licking a tiny patch of whipped cream from her lips? Although *sexy* was far too mundane a word for his primitive and overwhelming need to possess her; or for the sensation he had of plummeting completely out of control to a destination unknown to him. Every nerve on edge, every sense finely honed. For underneath it all, wasn't he frightened?

Frightened? Him, Slade Carruthers? Of a woman?

"Aren't you going to eat anything, Slade?"

"What? Oh, sorry, of course I am." He took a square from the chased silver platter and bit into it. It was a date square. He hated date squares. He said, "The summer my mother learned how to make chocolate éclairs, my father and I each gained five pounds."

"Where did you grow up?"

"Manhattan. My parents still live there. My mother's on a health kick now, though. Soy burgers and salads."

"And what does your father think of that?"

"He eats them because he adores her. Then at least once a

week he takes her out for dinner in SoHo or Greenwich Village and plies her with wine and decadent desserts." Slade's face softened. "The next day it's back to tofu and radicchio."

"It sounds idyllic."

The sharpness in her voice would have cut paper. "You don't sound amused."

"I'm not a believer in marital bliss, whether flavored with tofu or chocolate," she said coldly. "Ah, there's Belle...if you'll excuse me, I must speak to her before I leave. I'll see you tomorrow."

She plunked her half-empty cup on the linen tablecloth so hard that tea slopped into the saucer. Then she threaded her way through the crowd toward Belle, her hair like a beacon among the clusters of pastel hats. Slade watched her go. *Prickly* wasn't the word for Clea Chardin.

Although she claimed never to have been married, some guy had sure pulled a dirty on her. Recently, by the sound of things, and far from superficially.

He'd like to kill the bastard.

Maybe Belle would fill him in on the details at dinner tonight. After a couple of glasses of her favorite Pinot Noir.

He wanted to know everything there was to know about Clea Chardin.

CHAPTER TWO

THAT evening, Slade waited until he and Belle were halfway through their grilled squab, in a trendy French restaurant on Nob Hill, before saying, "I met Clea Chardin at your party this afternoon, Belle."

Belle's fork stopped in midair. While her hair was unabashedly gray, her shantung evening suit was pumpkin-orange, teamed with yellow diamonds that sparkled in the candlelight. Her eyes, enlarged with lime-green mascara, were shrewd: Belle harbored no illusions about human nature. Slade was one of the few people who knew how much of her fortune went to medical clinics for the indigent.

"Delightful gal, Clea," she said.

"Tell me about her."

"Why, Slade?"

"She interests me," he hedged.

"In that case, I'll leave her to do the telling," Belle said. "The sauce is delicious, isn't it?"

"So that's your last word?"

"Don't play games with Clea. That's my last word."

"I'm not in the habit of playing games!"

"No? You're thirty-five years old, unmarried, hugely rich and very sexy…why hasn't some woman snagged you before now?" Belle answered her own question. "Because you know all the moves and you're adept at keeping your distance. I'm telling you, don't trifle with Clea Chardin."

"She struck me as someone who can look after herself."

"So she's a good actor."

Belle looked distinctly ruffled. Choosing not to ask why Clea was so defenseless, Slade took another mouthful of the rich meat and chewed thoughtfully. "Maggie Yarrow was in fine form," he said.

Belle gave an uncouth cackle. "Don't know why I invite her, she gets more outrageous every year. Nearly decapitated one of my waiters with that cane of hers...which reminds me, did you see what the senator's wife was wearing? Looked like she ransacked the thrift shop."

He knew better than to ask why Belle had slackened her infamous dress code for Clea. "Will your lawn recover from all those stiletto heels?"

"A whole generation of women crippled," Belle said grandly. "What's a patch of grass compared to that?"

He raised his glass. "To next year's party."

She gave him the sweet smile that came rarely and that he cherished. "You be sure to be here, won't you, Slade? I count on it."

"I will."

His affairs never lasted more than six months; so by then, he'd no longer be seeing Clea. Game over.

Oddly, he felt a sharp pang of regret.

The next morning Slade was walking along Pier 39 past the colorful moored fishing boats. It was October, sunniest month in the city, and tourists still thronged the boardwalk, along with buskers joking raucously with the crowds. The tall spire of the carousel beckoned to him, the lilt of its music teasing his ears. Would Clea be there? Or would she have thought the better of it and remained in her hotel?

He had no idea where she was staying. Added to that, she was going back to Europe tomorrow. If she was determined not to be found, Europe was a big place.

He walked the circumference of the fence surrounding the carousel, his eyes darting this way and that. No Clea. She'd changed her mind, he thought, angered that she should trifle with him. But underlying anger was a depth of disappointment that dismayed him.

Then movement caught his eye. A woman was waving to him. It was Clea, seated on the gold-painted sidesaddle of a high-necked horse, clasping the decorated pole as she went slowly up and down. He waved back, the tension in his shoulders relaxing.

She'd come. The rest was up to him.

The brim of her huge, flower-bedecked sun hat flopped up and down with the horse's movements. Her legs were bare, pale against her mount's dark flanks. Bare. Long. Slender.

As the carousel came to a stop, she slid to the floor. She was wearing a wildly flowered skirt that fell in soft folds around her thighs, a clinging top in a green so vivid it hurt his eyes and matching green flat-heeled sandals. The skirt should be banned, Slade thought. Or was he even capable of thought through a surge of lust unlike any he'd ever known?

Clea walked toward Slade, her heart jittering in her chest. He was so overpoweringly male, she thought. Tall, broad-shouldered, long-legged, with an aura of power that she was almost sure he was unaware of, and which in consequence was all the more effective. She came to a halt two feet away from him. *"Buon giorno."*

"Come sta?"

"Molto bene, grazie." She gave him a dazzling smile that

reduced his brain to mush. "This is a fun place, Slade, I'm glad you suggested it."

"Popsicles," he said firmly, and led her to the little booth decorated with big bunches of rainbow-hued balloons.

She chose grape, he raspberry. Sucking companionably, they wandered in and out of the boutiques and stands, Slade purposely keeping the conversation light. Belle was no fool, and had, in her way, only confirmed his own suspicions: Clea had been badly burned and it behooved him to take it slow.

Slow? When she went back to Europe tomorrow?

Slow. He made frequent trips to Europe.

They watched a very talented mime artist, and a somewhat less talented musician, tossing coins into their hats. Out of the blue Clea said, "Did you enjoy your dinner with Belle?"

"I did, yes. We go back a long way—she's known my parents for years."

"Ah yes, your estimable parents."

"I like my parents and I'm not about to apologize for it," Slade said, a matching edge to his voice.

"It's none of my business how you feel about them."

He reached over and wiped a drop of purple from her mouth with his fingertip. "Why don't you believe in marital harmony?"

As she bit her lip, it was as much as he could do to keep his hands at his sides. "I told you—I'm a realist. Oh look, what gorgeous earrings."

She dragged him over to a kiosk selling abalone earrings that shimmered turquoise and pink. Lifting one to her ear, she said, "What do you think?"

"They clash with your sweater. But you could wear anything, and you'd still look devastatingly beautiful." Anything, he thought. Or nothing.

She laughed. "Oh, you Americans—so direct. The earrings, Slade, the earrings."

"They match your eyes. Let me buy them for you."

"So I'll be indebted?"

"So I'll have the pleasure of knowing that perhaps, occasionally, you'll think of me."

"I promise that perhaps, occasionally, I will," she said, removing the gold hoops she was wearing and tucking them in her purse. Increasingly, she was finding it difficult not to like Slade. Didn't that make him all the more of a threat?

"Let me," Slade said, and with exquisite care inserted the silver hooks into her lobes. Her skin was as smooth as he'd imagined it. Deep within him, desire shuddered into life.

Her irises had darkened, as though a cloud had covered the sea. He stepped back, reaching for his wallet and paying for the earrings. "They look great on you."

She struggled to find her voice. "Thank you."

"My pleasure," he said formally.

Between them, unspoken, crackled the electric awareness of sexual attraction. Slade said abruptly, "You know I want you. You've probably known it from the first moment we met."

"Yes, of course I know—which doesn't mean we do anything about it…other than enjoy each other's company on a sunny morning in October." She fluttered her lashes at him in deliberate parody. "Are you enjoying my company?"

"Very much. Don't fish, Clea."

"Where better than on Fisherman's Wharf?" As he chuckled, she went on calmly, "We're talking about sex between two total strangers here. Possibility is so often more interesting than actuality, wouldn't you agree?"

"Not when one of the strangers is you."

"You have a pretty way with a compliment."

He said, fixing her with his gaze, "Possibility's on a par

with fantasy. Nothing wrong with fantasy—last night I had a few about you I'd be embarrassed to describe. But actuality is real. Real and risky. That's the catch, isn't it?"

She said through gritted teeth, "I don't sleep with someone I don't know."

"That's easily fixable. We can get to know each other."

"Slade, I've been told I'm beautiful, and I know I'm rich. Consequently I've learned to choose my partners carefully. I already told you that you scare me—you're the last man I'd have an affair with."

He shouldn't have been so direct. But he had a horrible sense of time running out, along with the even worse sense that nothing he was saying to her was making any real or lasting impression. Welcome to a new experience, Slade thought wryly. He'd never before had to work at getting a woman interested in him; fighting them off was his area of expertise.

"There's a bakery a couple of blocks from here that sells crusty sourdough bread," he said. "I always take some home with me."

He heard the tiny puff as she let out her breath. "Let's go," she said agreeably. "Do you like to cook?"

"I do. Sheer self-defense. I eat out a lot, and it's relaxing to stay home and cook for myself. My specialties are bouillabaisse and pumpkin pie. I'll make them for you sometime."

"Perhaps. Occasionally," she said, her eyes full of mockery.

"For sure. At least once."

"You don't like opposition."

"Neither, dear Clea, do you."

She laughed. "Who does? Tell me about sourdough bread—it doesn't sound very appetizing."

Impatient of small talk, suddenly desperate for details beyond the superficial, Slade said, "How old are you, Clea?"

"Old enough to enjoy flirtation without—how do you say

it?—strings attached." She stepped off the boardwalk onto the sidewalk at the end of the wharf. "As for—"

Shouting and swearing, a gang of teenagers surged around the nearest building. Three of them collided head-on with Slade. Automatically he threw his arms around Clea, pulling her close to his body for protection, his feet planted hard on the tarmac.

"Sorry!" one of the kids yelled. Another gave a loud whoop. None of them stopped.

Slade stood very still. Clea's body was crushed to his, her breasts jammed against his chest. One of his arms encircled her hips, the other her waist; for a heart-stopping moment he felt her yield to him.

Her floppy hat had been shoved to the back of her head. He bent his own head and found her lips in a kiss that he wanted to last forever.

And again she yielded to him, a surrender all the more potent for being unexpected. He brought one hand up, tangling it in her hair, so silky and sweet-scented, and deepened the kiss, his lips edging hers apart. Her fingers were digging into his nape; her tongue was laced with his, teasing him, tasting him, driving him out of his mind.

As animal hunger surged through him, he forgot he was on a city sidewalk; forgot all Belle's warnings and his own advice. Robbed of any vestige of caution, he muttered, "I feel as though I've been waiting for you my whole life…God, how I want you!"

His words sliced through the frantic pulsing of Clea's blood, and brought in their wake an ice-cold dash of reality. She stiffened, then pushed hard against Slade's chest. "Stop!" she gasped. "What are we thinking of?"

"We're not thinking at all, which is just the way it should be," he said thickly, lifting her chin with his fingers and bending to kiss her again.

"Slade, stop—you mustn't, I don't want you to."

His gaze bored into hers. "Yes, you do."

She sagged in his embrace, her forehead resting on his chest. He was right. She had wanted him, in the most basic of ways, her body betraying her into a response that, in retrospect, appalled her. "You took me by surprise, that's all," she said weakly.

Keeping one arm around her waist, he said, "We're going into a restaurant on the pier, we're having lunch together and we're talking this through. No perhaps, no opposition."

All the fight had gone out of her; she looked both frightened and defenseless. Slade hardened his heart and headed back along the pier to a restaurant that specialized in seafood. Because they were early for lunch, he was able to get a table in one corner, overlooking the bay. A table with a degree of privacy, he thought, and sat down across from her.

She picked up the menu; to his consternation, he saw how she had to rest it on the table to disguise the trembling of her hands. But by the time she looked up, she had herself under control again. Unsmiling, she said, "I'll have the sole."

Quickly he ordered their food, along with a bottle of Chardonnay from a Napa Valley vineyard. The service was fast; within minutes he was raising his glass of chilled pale golden wine. "To international relations," he said with a crooked smile.

Her mouth set, she said, "To international boundaries," and took a big gulp of wine. Putting her glass down, she said, "Slade, let's get this out of the way, then maybe we can go back to enjoying each other's company. What happened out there on the sidewalk—it frightened me. I don't want a repeat, nor do I want to discuss the reasons you frighten me. And, of course, it simply confirmed what I've already told you—I'm not available. No sex. No affair. Is that understood?"

Banking his anger, Slade said curtly, "Of course it's not understood—how could it be when I have no idea why I frighten you? It's certainly not my intent to do so."

"I didn't say it was." She took another reckless gulp of wine. "We're strangers—and strangers we'll remain. That's all I'm saying."

"I want far more than that."

"We don't always get what we want. You're old enough to know that."

"You kissed me back, Clea. And I'm going to get what I want."

Heat flushed her cheeks. "No, you're not." Quickly she reached for her purse. It was time to produce her usual line of defense with a man who wouldn't take no for an answer. Hadn't she known when she'd left the hotel this morning that she'd need it with Slade Carruthers?

Taking out an envelope, she plunked it on the table. "You should take a look at this."

"Are you about to ruin my appetite?" he said.

"Just look at it, Slade."

The envelope was full of clippings from various tabloids and newspapers the width of Europe. Clea was pictured in every article, hair up, hair down, in evening gowns and jewels, in skimpy bikinis, in jeans and boots. Accompanied by, Slade saw, a succession of men. Aristocrats, artists, businessmen: none of them looking at all unhappy to be escorting the rich, the elegant, the charming Clea Chardin.

"What are you trying to tell me?" he said carefully.

"What does it look like?"

"Like you date a lot of different men."

"Date?" she repeated, lifting one brow.

"Are you trying to tell me you've slept with all of them?"

"Not all of them, no," she said. It was the truth, but not the entire truth. She should have said, "With none of them." But a reputation for flitting from man to man was, at times, extremely useful; right now she needed every weapon she could lay her hands on.

The waiter put their plates in front of them, said, "Enjoy," and left them alone again.

Clea said, as if there'd been no interruption, "If you want to take me to bed, you should know what you're getting into. I date lots of men and that's the way I like it."

Her hair shimmered in the light. Slade flicked the clippings with his finger. "So I'd be just one more guy to add to the list."

"You don't have to keep on seeing me if you don't like the way I operate," she said mildly.

He didn't like it. At all. "Are you saying if we had an affair, you wouldn't be faithful to me for its duration?"

"That's the general idea," she said, wondering why she should feel so ashamed of her duplicity when she was achieving her aim: to send Slade Carruthers in the opposite direction as quickly as she could.

Slade looked down at his *cioppino*. He wasn't the slightest bit hungry. Picking up his spoon, he said, "I happen to have a few standards. I'm not into long-term commitment or marriage, but when I have a relationship with a woman I expect fidelity, and I promise the same."

She shrugged. "Then let's enjoy our lunch and say goodbye."

He said with dangerous softness, "Perhaps I could change your mind. On the subject of standards."

"You're not going to get the chance."

"I make frequent trips to Europe. If we exchange e-mail addresses, we can keep in touch and arrange to meet some time."

She was attacking her sole as though she couldn't wait to

be rid of him. "No. Which, as I'm sure you know, is spelled identically in English and Italian."

He'd never begged a woman for anything in his life. He wasn't going to start with Clea Chardin. "Commitment is what you're really avoiding. Why?"

Clea put down her knife and fork and looked right at him, her remarkable eyes brilliant with sincerity. "I don't want to hurt you, Slade. And hurt you I would, were you to pursue me, because—as you just pointed out—our standards are different. So I'm ending this now, before it begins."

He said sharply, "I don't let women close enough to hurt me."

Her temper flared. "Why am I not surprised?"

"You must have hurt some of those other men."

"They knew the score and were willing to go along with me."

Cut your losses, Slade thought. Get out with some dignity. What's the alternative? Grovel?

Not your style.

Biting off his words, anger rising like bile in his throat, Slade said, "So you're going to play it safe. Ignore that kiss as if it never happened."

With a huge effort Clea kept her eyes trained on his. "That's right."

"Then there's nothing more to say." Picking up his spoon, he choked down a mouthful of the rich tomato broth.

She was eating her fish as fast as she could. She hadn't lost her appetite, Slade thought sourly. Why should she? He didn't matter a whit to her.

Rationally he should be admiring her for turning her back so decisively on all his money. Unfortunately he felt about as rational as a shipwrecked sailor brought face-to-face with Miss America.

Clea drained her wine. "You're sulking."

He put his spoon down with exaggerated care. "If you

don't know the difference between sulking and genuine passion, you're worse off than I suspected."

She paled. Surely he hadn't guessed that she'd never known genuine passion? Reaching in her purse, she extracted a bill, tossed it on the table and said coldly, "That's to pay for my lunch. Goodbye, Slade."

Pushing back her chair, she walked away from him, her hips swaying in her flowered skirt. With an effort that made him break out into a cold sweat, Slade stayed where he was, his fingernails digging into the chair. Be damned if he'd chase after her.

He picked up his glass, tossed back the contents and addressed his seafood stew. He would never in his life order *cioppino* again.

He'd never go to bed with Clea Chardin, either: if it came to a battle of wills, he was going to be the one in control. Not her. So he'd better forget the highly erotic fantasies that had disturbed his sleep all night.

The empty chair across from him was no fantasy, nor was the twenty-dollar bill lying beside Clea's plate. The money felt like the final insult.

He'd give it to the first panhandler he met.

Through the plate glass window, Slade watched the waters of the bay sparkle in the sunshine. He felt as though he'd been presented with a jewel of outstanding brilliance. But before he could touch it, it had been snatched from his reach.

CHAPTER THREE

AT THREE o'clock that afternoon in his hotel room, Slade was on the telephone punching in Sarah Hutchinson's extension. Sarah was Belle's cook, whom Slade had known for years, and whose chocolate truffles he liked almost as much as he liked her. When she answered, he said, "Sarah, it's Slade Carruthers."

"Mr. Slade, what a nice surprise...how are you?"

They chatted for a few minutes about the garden party, then Slade said easily, "I've mislaid my appointment book—Mrs. Hayward's having dinner with Clea Chardin tonight, isn't she?" He waited for her reply, his heart thumping so loudly he was afraid she'd hear it over the phone.

"That's right. Seven o'clock."

"Just the two of them?"

"Private, that's what Mrs. Hayward said."

"Great—I'll call Belle in the morning, then. No need to mention this, Sarah, she'll think I'm having a memory lapse. How are your grandchildren?"

He patiently listened to their many virtues, then hung up. All he had to do now was decide on a course of action. Gatecrash Belle's place? Or find a bar, get royally drunk and cut his losses?

Slade started prowling up and down the room, as restless as a caged tiger. Why had he phoned Sarah Hutchinson? Why couldn't he—for once in his life—accept that a woman didn't want to go to bed with him?

The answer was simple: because he wanted Clea as he'd never wanted a woman before.

Or was it that simple? Clea had been so ardent in his arms, then so frightened by her own response. Neither reaction had been fake, he'd swear to it. By touching her physically, he'd touched her emotions in a way that had terrified her.

So she'd very cleverly produced the clippings, refused any prospect of fidelity and taken her leave. She'd played him, he thought. And he'd fallen for it.

It wasn't going to happen again. Be damned if he was going to sit back and let Clea Chardin vanish from his life. He wanted her and he was going to have her. On his terms.

All of which meant he'd better have a plan of action in mind before nine-thirty tonight.

At nine-thirty, however, when Slade pressed the heavy brass bell on the Hayward front door, he felt devoid of anything that could be called a plan. He'd have to wing it. But this time he'd be the one in control.

Carter, the butler, let him in and left him in the formal parlor, where family photographs in sterling silver frames covered every available surface. The furniture represented, in Slade's opinion, the very worst of Victorian excess. Over the elaborate wrought-iron fireplace, a stuffed stag's head gazed down its aristocratic nose at him.

There was a painting by the fireplace, a small dark oil. Curious, he wandered over to look at it. A man in chains, head bowed in utter defeat, was being led by three armored guards into the black maw of a cave. Slade knew, instantly, that the prisoner would never emerge into daylight again.

It was his own lasting nightmare, he thought, his palms damp, his fingers curled into fists: the nightmare that had tormented him ever since he was eleven. His limbs heavy as lead, he turned away from the painting, staring instead at an innocuous watercolor of a sunny meadow.

"Slade," Belle exclaimed, "is anything wrong? Your parents? You look terrible!"

He fought to banish the nightmare where it belonged, deep down in his psyche. While Belle knew the reason behind it, she had no idea of its extent, and he wasn't about to enlighten her. "I didn't mean to frighten you," he said with real compunction. "My parents are fine. I'm here because I need to see Clea."

Her smile vanishing as if it had been wiped from her face, Belle said, "How did you know she's here?"

"I got it out of Sarah and you're not to blame her. Clea and I had lunch today, Belle. But we left some loose ends about our next meeting. I head off to Japan tomorrow and she's going back to Europe, so I figured it was simplest if I turned up on your doorstep and gave her a lift back to her hotel."

Tonight Belle was wearing a rust-brown linen dress that did little for her complexion. Rubies gleamed in her earlobes. She looked like a highly suspicious rooster, Slade thought with a quiver of amusement, and said truthfully, "I don't want Clea to disappear from my life—there's something about her that really turns my crank."

Belle said flatly, "If she doesn't want to drive to the hotel with you, I'm not pushing her."

He hesitated. "She dates a lot of men, so she told me. But when I kissed her, she acted like a scared rabbit. Do you have any idea why?"

"If I did, do you think I'd tell you?"

"I'm not out to hurt her, Belle."

"Then maybe you'd better head right out the front door."

He said tightly, "You've known me since I was knee-high to a grasshopper. Have you ever seen me chase after a woman before?"

"I've seen you treat women as though they're ornaments sitting on a shelf—decorative enough, but not really worth your full attention."

He winced. "Clea gets my full attention just by being in the same room. So she's different from the rest."

"That's what they all say."

"You're an old friend, and I'm asking you to trust me," Slade said, any amusement long gone. "Clea's knocked me right off balance. No other woman's ever come close to doing that. All I want is the chance to drive her back to her hotel—I'm not going to jump on her the minute she gets in the car!"

"And if she says no?"

"She won't."

Belle snapped, "If you hurt that gal, I'll—I won't invite you to next year's garden party."

It was a dire threat. "Belle, I'll go out on a limb here. I want Clea, no question of that, but I have this gut feeling she's not really running away from me, she's running from herself. And I don't give a damn if that sounds presumptuous."

For a long moment Belle simply stared at him. Then she said, "I'll ask her if she wants a drive back to her hotel."

The massive oak door swung shut behind her. The stag's upper lip sneered down at him. Turning his back on the dark little oil painting, Slade jammed his hands in his pockets and stared down at the priceless, rose-embroidered carpet. He felt like his life were hanging in the balance.

How melodramatic was that? Sex was all he wanted. Nothing more. Nothing less.

Five minutes later—he timed it on his watch—the door was pushed open. Clea marched through, followed by Belle in her rust-brown dress. Clea's dress was ice-pale turquoise, calf-length, fashioned out of soft jersey; her hair had been tamed into a coil on the back of her head. With a physical jolt, Slade saw she was still wearing the earrings he'd given her earlier in the day.

Clea said crisply, "I said goodbye to you this morning."

"It wasn't goodbye. More like *au revoir.*"

"My hotel is exactly four blocks from here—I can walk."

"If you won't go with me, you're going in a cab."

Clea glared at him, then transferred that glare to Belle. "This man is your friend?"

Belle said calmly, "If he wasn't, he wouldn't have made it past the front door."

Clea's breath hissed between her teeth. When had she ever felt as angry as she did now? Angry, afraid, cornered and—treacherously, underneath it all—ridiculously happy to see Slade. Happy? When the man threatened to knock down the whole house of cards that was her life? "All right, Slade, you can drive me to my hotel," she said. "But only because I don't want to waste my time arguing with you."

"Fine," he said, unable to subdue his grin.

She said furiously, "Your smile should be banned—lethal to any female over the age of twelve."

Belle smothered a snort of laughter. "You've got to admit he's cute, Clea."

"Cute?" Slade said, wincing.

"Cute like a high voltage wire is cute," Clea snapped.

"Certainly plenty of voltage between the two of you," Belle remarked, leading the way to the front door, where she took a lacy shawl from the cupboard and passed it to Slade. Dry-mouthed, he draped it over Clea's shoulders.

Belle leaned forward to kiss Clea on the cheek. "We'll talk next week."

"Monday or Tuesday." Clea's voice softened. "Thank you, Belle."

"Slade's a good man," Belle added.

Clea's smile was ironic. "Maybe I prefer bad men."

Slade said in a voice like steel, "Good, bad or indifferent, I really dislike being discussed as though I don't exist."

Belle said lightly, "Indifferent wouldn't apply to either one of you. Good night."

Slade and Clea stepped out into the cool darkness, which was still scented with roses, and the door closed behind them. He reached over and plucked a pale yellow bloom; she stood as still as one of the marble statues flanking the driveway as he tucked it into her hair. "I think that'll stay," he said, tugging on the stem.

Her eyes were like dark pools. "You're a hopeless romantic."

"You're still wearing the abalone earrings," he retorted. "Doesn't that make you one as well?"

"They go with my dress."

"We're arguing again."

"How unromantic," she said. As he helped her into his rented car, a speedy silver Porsche, the slit in her skirt bared her legs in their iridescent hose. Taking her time, she tucked her feet under the dash, straightened her skirt and smiled up at him. "Thank you," she said with perfect composure.

Slade took a deep breath, shut her door and marched around to the driver's seat. His next job was to convince her that he was going to become her lover. And by God, he was going to succeed.

"I'll buy you a drink at the hotel," he said, and turned onto the street.

By now, Clea had managed to gather her thoughts. It was time for her second line of defense, she decided. One she would have no scruples using with Slade. She called it; privately, The

Test, and it had rarely failed her. She was certain it would work with Slade Carruthers, a man used to wielding power and being in command. "A drink would be nice," she said.

"That was easy."

"I dislike being predictable."

"You don't have a worry in the world."

He'd made it past the first hurdle, Slade thought, and concentrated on his driving. After leaving the car with the hotel valet, he led her into the opulent lobby. Marble, mahogany, oriental carpeting and a profusion of tropical blooms declared without subtlety that no expense had been spared. He said, "I would have thought something less ostentatious would have been more to your liking."

"Belle made the reservations."

It was definitely Belle's kind of place. In the bar, a jazz singer was crooning, her hands wandering the keys of the grand piano. They made their way to a table near the dark red velvet curtains with their silken tassels. The ceiling was scrolled in gold, the walls layered in damask of the same deep red.

Waiting until the waiter had brought their drinks, Slade said, "The clippings you showed me this morning threw me, Clea, as no doubt you intended. Nor did I like your terms. But I gave up much too easily."

She took a delicate sip of her martini. "You're used to women chasing you."

"I have a lot of money—it's a powerful aphrodisiac."

She raised her brows. "Now who's the cynic?"

He leaned forward, speaking with all the force of his personality. "Clea, I want you in my bed…and I'm convinced that you want to be there, too. I travel a lot, we can meet anywhere you like."

Clea said evenly, hating herself for the lie, "I play the field, I have a good time and move on. That's what I told you this morning, and it hasn't changed. You can give me your phone number, if you like—and if I'm ever at a loose end, I'll call you."

So she was lumping him together with what she called, so amorphously, *the field*. Slade said, lifting one brow, "I dare you to make a date with me. More than that, I dare you to get to know me. In bed and out."

Her nostrils flared. "You're being very childish."

"Am I? If we stop taking risks, something in us dies."

"Risks can kill!"

"I assure you, I don't have homicide in mind." *Kill,* he thought. That's a strong word.

Her breasts rising and falling with her agitated breathing, Clea said, "Men don't stick around long enough for women to get to know them."

"Generalizations are the sign of a lazy mind."

"The first sign of trouble, you'll be gone faster than I can say *au revoir.*"

"You're being both sexist and cowardly," he said.

Her chin snapped up. "Who gave you the right to stand in judgment on me?"

"Deny it, then."

"I'm not a coward!"

Slade said softly, "Prove it to me. More important, prove it to yourself."

Toying with the olive in her glass, Clea said raggedly, "You're talking about us getting to know each other. Yet you never let any of your women close enough to hurt you."

He said grimly, "You may be the exception that proves the rule."

And how was she supposed to interpret that? "I like my life the way it is," she said. "Why should I change?"

"If you didn't want to change, we wouldn't be sitting here having this conversation."

He was wrong. Completely wrong. "Do you do this with every woman you meet?"

"I've never had to before."

"So why are you bothering now?"

"Clea, I don't want to play the field," he said forcibly. "Right now it's you I want. You, exclusively. Because deep down I don't really believe you are a coward."

"Just sexist," she said with a flare of defiance.

"Don't you get bored playing the field?"

She said nastily, "I've not, so far, been bored with you."

"Then I'll make another dare—date me until you do get bored." Slade pushed a piece of paper across the table to her. "My personal assistant's phone number in New York. His name's Bill and he always knows where I can be reached."

She stared down at the paper as if it might rear up and bite her. Her second line of defense, she thought wildly, what had happened to it? Hadn't Slade jumped in ahead of her, daring her to date him? Worse, to go to bed with him? "I'm not interested in your money," she blurted, trying to collect her wits. "I have plenty of my own."

"I never thought you were."

The Test, she thought. Now's the time. Do it, Clea. She glanced up, her accent pronounced, as it always was when she was upset. "Very well, Slade...I also can make dares."

"Go ahead."

"Meet me in the Genoese Bar in Monte Carlo, three weeks from now. In the evening, anytime after seven-thirty. Wednesday, Thursday or Friday."

"Name the day," he said.

"Ah," she said smoothly, "that's part of the dare. I'm not telling you which evening. Either I'm worth waiting for, or I'm not—which is it?"

"But you will turn up?"

Her eyes flashed fire. "I give my word."

"Then I'll wait for you."

"It stays open until 2:00 a.m., and the music is deafening," she said with a malicious smile. "You won't wait. No man would. Not when the world's full of beautiful women who are instantly available."

"You underrate yourself," he said softly. Reaching over with his finger, he traced the soft curve of her mouth until her lip trembled. "I'll wait."

Fear flickered along her nerves. He wouldn't wait. Not Slade Carruthers, who—she'd swear—had never had to wait for a woman in his life. Tossing her head, she said, "If you're unfamiliar with Monte Carlo, anyone can direct you to the Genoese—it's well known."

"Monte Carlo—where life's a gamble and the stakes are high."

"High stakes? For you, maybe—not for me." Which was another barefaced lie.

"I wouldn't be where I am today if I didn't know how to gamble, Clea…tomorrow I'll give Bill your name. You have only to mention it, and he'll make sure I get any messages from you."

She said, so quietly that the drifting jazz melody almost drowned her out, "I must be mad to have suggested a meeting between us. Even one you won't keep."

She looked exhausted. Slade drained his whisky. "Finish up," he said, "and I'll take you back to the lobby. Then I'll be on my way—my flight's early tomorrow."

Her face unreadable, she said, "So you're not putting the moves on me tonight?"

His jaw tightened. "I don't gamble when the deck's stacked against me—that's plain stupidity."

"At any table, you'd make a formidable opponent."

He pushed back his chair. "I'll take that as a compliment. Come on, you look wiped."

"Wiped? I don't know what that means, but it doesn't sound flattering."

He took her hand and brought her to her feet. Standing very close to her, his eyes caressing her features, he said huskily, "It means tired out. In need of a good night's sleep. When you and I share a bed, sleep won't be the priority."

"*When* we share a bed?" she said, looking full at him. "I've never liked being taken for granted."

His eyes were a compelling midnight-blue, depthless and inscrutable. Charismatic eyes, which pulled her to him as though she had no mind of her own. She felt herself sway toward him, the ache of desire blossoming deep in her belly and making nonsense of all her defenses. Reaching up, she brushed his lips with hers as lightly as the touch of a butterfly's wing, then just as quickly stepped back.

Her heart was hammering in her breast. So much for keeping him at a distance, she thought, aghast. What was wrong with her?

For once Slade found himself bereft of speech. Going on impulse, he lifted her hand to his lips and kissed it with lingering pleasure, watching color flare in her cheeks. Then, calling on all his control, he looped one arm lightly around her shoulders and led her back to the lobby. The light from the crystal chandeliers seemed excessively bright. He said, "The Genoese. In three weeks. If you need anything in the meantime, call me."

"I won't call you," Clea said. Turning on her heel, she crossed the vast carpet to the elevators.

Nor did she.

CHAPTER FOUR

THE Genoese Bar on a cool damp evening in November should have been a welcome destination. Slade had walked from his hotel, with its magnificent view of the Port of Monaco and the choppy Mediterranean, past the obsessively groomed gardens of the casino to a curving side street near the water where a discreetly lit sign announced the Genoese. It was exactly seven-thirty.

The bar, he saw with a sinking heart, was underground, down a flight of narrow, winding stairs.

His nightmare, once again.

He was thirty-five years old now. Not eleven. He should be able to walk down a flight of stairs and spend six hours in a windowless room without hyperventilating.

Yeah, right.

Clea, he was almost sure, wouldn't arrive until Friday. If this was some sort of test, why would she meet him any sooner? Unless she thought he wouldn't bother turning up until Friday, and in consequence came tonight.

It was useless trying to second-guess her. Taking a deep breath of the salt-laden air, Slade walked slowly down the stairs and pushed open the heavy, black-painted door.

The noise hit him like a blow. Rap, played as loud as

the sound equipment could handle it. He'd never been a fan of rap.

He let the door shut behind him, his heart thudding in his chest. The room was vast, tables all around its circumference, a small dance floor in the center under flickering strobes that instantly disoriented him. A big room, he thought crazily. Not cupboard-size, like the one he'd never been able to forget.

Come on, buddy, you can do this.

Leaning against the wall, he let his gaze travel from face to face, wishing with all his heart that Clea's would be among them. It was a young crowd, in expensive leather and designer jeans, the women's silky hair gleaming like shampoo ads, the energy level frenetic.

Clea was nowhere to be seen.

Slade claimed an empty table near the door, where he could see anyone who entered or left. Shucking off his trench coat, he sat down and ordered a bottle of Merlot and a dish of nuts. Automatically he located the Exit signs, wishing the ceiling didn't feel so low, wishing they'd turn off the strobe lights. Wishing that he'd never met Clea Chardin.

His hormones were ruling his life, he thought savagely. How he resented the hold she had on him, with her slender body and exquisite face! But no matter how fiercely he'd fought the strength of that hold, he couldn't dislodge it. God knows he'd tried hard enough the last three weeks.

She, in all fairness, had no idea how arduous a test she'd devised for him by making him wait in an underground bar.

As the array of bottles at the mirrored bar splintered and flashed in the strobes, dancers writhed to the primitive, undoubtedly hostile music. The little underground room had been quiet. Dead quiet. Frighteningly, maddeningly quiet.

All these years later, Slade still did his best never to think about the kidnapping that had so altered his life. At age eleven, he'd been snatched from the sidewalk near his school, drugged and kept in darkness in a small room below the ground, for a total of fifteen days and fourteen nights.

The kidnappers, he'd learned later, had been demanding ransom. The FBI, working with admirable flair and efficiency, had tracked down the hiding place, taken the kidnappers into custody and rescued him. Apart from the drugs, aimed at keeping him quiet and administered from a syringe by a masked man who never spoke to him, he was unharmed.

He'd never forgotten his mother's silent tears when she'd been brought face-to-face with him at the police station, or the deeply carved lines in his father's face.

The lasting aftereffect had been a phobia for dark, underground spaces. Right now, to his mortification, his palms were damp, his throat tight and his heart bouncing around in his chest. Just like when he was eleven.

A woman in a black leather jerkin and miniskirt sidled up to his table. Pouting her red lips, she said over the thud of the bass, "Want to dance?"

So she'd picked him out as an American. "No, thanks," he said.

She leaned forward, presenting him with an impressive cleavage. "You didn't come here to be alone."

"I'm waiting for someone," he said in a clipped voice. "I'd prefer to do that alone. Sorry."

Smoothing the leather over her hips, she shrugged. "Change your mind, I'm over by the bar."

By 2:00 a.m., when the bouncer closed the bar, Slade had been propositioned six times, felt permanently deafened and was heartily tired of Merlot and peanuts. His claustrophobia had not noticeably abated.

He climbed the stairs and emerged onto the sidewalk. Thrusting his hands in his pockets, he strode east along the waterfront, where buildings crowded down the hillside to a pale curve of sand. Useless to think of sleeping until he'd walked off those agonizingly long hours.

He should leave Monaco. Forget this whole ridiculous venture. Was any woman worth two more evenings in the Genoese Bar? After all, what did he really know about Clea? Sure, she'd given her word. But was it worth anything? What if she didn't show up? What if she'd spent the evening in Milan with one of the many men she'd mentioned, laughing to herself at the thought of Slade sitting in a crowded bar on the Riviera in November?

She was making a fool of him. He hated that as much as he hated being confronted by the demons of his past.

And how could he lust after a woman whose sexual standards, to put it mildly, were by no means exacting? Promiscuous, he thought heavily, and knew it was a word he'd been repressing for the last three weeks.

She looked so angelic, yet she'd slept with men the length and breadth of Europe. The clippings and her own admission proved it.

He should fly back to New York in the morning and forget the redhead with the vivid eyes, dancing intelligence and lax morals. Hadn't she done her best from the beginning to discourage him? The Genoese Bar was the final touch. After three nights of his life wasted in a futile vigil, he wouldn't be in any hurry to search her out.

Which meant, of course, that she'd won.

At three-thirty Slade's head hit the pillow; at five-forty-two he was jerked awake from a nightmare of a syringe impaling him to a dirty mattress; and at eight that evening, he was again descending the stairs of the Genoese Bar. Clea didn't show up that night, either. Nor had she appeared by one-thirty the following night.

By Friday Slade's vigil in the bar had become as much a test of his courage and endurance as anything to do with Clea. He was intent on proving to himself that he could stick it out for one more night; that the low ceiling and dark corners weren't able to drive him up the stairs in defeat.

That night he was drinking Cabernet Sauvignon. He had a headache, he was sleep-deprived, he was in a foul mood. He sure didn't feel the slightest bit romantic.

At one-forty, Clea walked down the stairs into the bar.

Slade eased well back into the shadows as she stood on the stairs looking around, her red hair in its usual wild swirl. Her jade-green evening suit boasted a silk camisole that clung to her breasts. He fought down a jolt of lust that infuriated him.

Be damned if he was going to fall at her feet in abject gratitude because she'd finally shown up.

From his stance against the wall he watched her search the room from end to end, checking out the men at the bar, the dancers, the seated, noisy crowd. On her face settled a look compounded of satisfaction, as though she'd proved her point, along with a sharp, and very real, regret.

The regret interested him rather more than he cared for.

Clea took the last of the stairs into the bar and wormed her way across the dance floor, her eyes darting this way and that. She couldn't see Slade anywhere. So he'd failed The Test. Given up. If indeed, he'd ever been here at all.

I'll wait, he'd said. But he'd lied.

A cold lump had settled in her chest. Hadn't she believed him when he'd said he'd wait for her? So, once again, her low opinion of the male of the species had been confirmed, rather more painfully than usual. She straightened her shoulders and tried to relax the tension in her jaw; when she reached the bar she ordered a glass of white wine and gave the room one more sweep.

Two men and a woman were edging toward her, old friends from Cannes; she hugged each of them, tossed back her wine and, with a defiant lift of her chin, walked out onto the dance floor with the taller of the two men.

Slade, watching, saw how the man's arm encompassed her waist, how his fingers were splayed over her hip. His anger rose another notch. *Playing the field...*her specialty.

He put his glass down on the table and strode across the room. Tapping the man on the shoulder, he said loudly, over the pounding rhythms of drums and bass guitars, "She's mine. Get lost."

Clea gave a shocked gasp. "Slade!"

"Did you think I wouldn't be here?" he said with disdain. "Tell your friend to vamoose. If he values living."

"I'll talk to you later, Stefan," she said, her heartbeat competing with the drums. "It's okay, I know Slade."

"On, no, you don't," Slade said, standing so close to her he could see a tiny fleck of mascara on her lower eyelid. "If you knew me, we wouldn't have had to indulge in this stupid charade."

"You agreed to it."

"You know what I want to do right now? Throw you over my shoulder, haul you out of this god-awful bar and carry you to the nearest bed."

He looked entirely capable of doing so. She said faintly, "Bouncers don't like it when you do things like that."

"It'd make me feel a whole lot better."

"I suggest we have a drink, instead."

"Scared of me, Clea?"

"Of a six foot two, one hundred ninety pound, extremely angry male? Why would I be scared?"

"I like you," he said.

She blinked. "Five seconds ago you looked as though you wanted to throttle me."

"Five minutes ago you looked extremely disappointed when you thought I wasn't here."

"You exaggerate!"

"I don't think so. Let's dance, Clea."

"Dance? With you? No way."

"I've sat in this bar for three long nights," he grated. "I've been propositioned, I've drunk inferior wine and I've been bored out of my skull. The least you can do is dance with me."

He'd waited for her. He'd passed The Test. Now what was she supposed to do? "You asked for it," she said recklessly.

The floor was crowded and the music raucous. Her eyes blazing with an emotion Slade couldn't possibly have named, Clea raised her arms above her head and threw back her mane of hair as movement rippled down her body. Lust stabbed his loins, hot and imperative. Holding her gaze with his, he matched her, move for move, and deliberately refrained from laying as much as a finger on her.

He didn't need to. Pagan as an ancient goddess, hips swaying, nipples thrusting against the thin silk of her camisole, Clea danced. Danced for him alone. Danced as though they were alone. Danced until he thought he might die of unfulfilled desire.

The music ended abruptly. Into the ringing silence, the barkeeper said, "Closing time, ladies and gentlemen."

Clea bit her lip, her breasts heaving. "You did it again," she whispered. "Made me forget who I am."

Slade dropped his hands to her shoulders and kissed her full on the mouth. "Good," he said. Dancing with her had also, for the space of four or five minutes, blanked out the fact that he was underground in a dark room.

Quite a woman, this Clea Chardin.

"Let's get out of here," she said. "I need some fresh air."

So did he. Slade took her firmly by the hand and led the way up the narrow stairs.

Outside, under a star-spattered sky, Clea took a long, steadying breath, trying to forget how wantonly she'd swayed and writhed on the dance floor. "I'm hungry," she said in faint surprise. "I forgot to eat dinner."

He'd been gulping air obsessively, hoping his enormous relief at being in the open air wouldn't show. But Clea said, puzzled, "What's the matter? Are you all right?"

He spoke the literal truth. "I spent far too long cooped up in that bar—not sure I've got any eardrums left." Tucking her hand in the crook of his elbow, he added, "Food—that'll help."

He set off at a killing pace along the brick sidewalk, which was lit by lamps atop curving iron posts. Distantly he could hear the soft shush of waves against the breakwater. A breeze rustled the tall cypresses, while palm fronds rattled and chattered edgily. Clea said breathlessly, "I said I was hungry, not starving. You could slow down."

"Sorry," he said, and moderated his pace. "How do you know Stefan?"

"I met him in Nice last year. He designs yachts for the very, very rich."

"Have you slept with him?"

"No."

"Do you own a yacht?"

She grinned. "I get seasick on a sheltered lagoon."

"But if you didn't, you could afford one of Stefan's yachts."

"My grandfather left me the bulk of his fortune. Payton Steel, have you heard of it?"

"Very, very rich," Slade said, tucking the name away in his mind. So her parents must be dead: a loss contributing to what he was beginning to suspect was a deep, underlying loneliness. Or was he way out to lunch? "Do you have any brothers or sisters?"

"No."

"So what do you do with your life, Clea? Other than play the field?"

"I have no need to do anything else."

He said, from a deep well of conviction that took him by surprise, "Don't give me that—you're far too intelligent to spend your life flitting from party to party."

They'd reached the floodlit façade of the casino, with its turrets and crenellations, its huge windows. The formal gardens were lit by tall lanterns; a fountain splashed in the light, the water falling like elegant bracelets of gold. Clea said tightly, "Where are we going to eat?"

"My hotel's five minutes from here. One of the restaurants is open all night."

"I'm not going to bed with you, Slade!"

"Just don't pretend you don't want to."

"It's a little late for that," she said irritably.

"You're damn right. Anyway, I didn't say room service, I said restaurant. Then I'll walk you straight back to your hotel."

"I leave here first thing in the morning."

"Covering all the angles, aren't you?" he said.

"I'm protecting myself—why wouldn't I?"

"You sure don't act like someone who goes from man to man, footloose and fancy-free."

"You're not like the rest!"

He stopped under one of the graceful street lamps, in front of a pink stucco house with charming iron-railed balconies and tall white shutters. "How am I different?"

"Too intense, too forceful, too—" she hesitated "—disturbing."

"Well, that's a start."

A red Ferrari roared past, drowning any reply she might have made. Tugging at his arm, she headed up the hill as if all the demons who'd assaulted him in the bar were after her. She had her own demons, he was convinced of it. He could have found out what they were with very little effort; one good private detective could unearth whatever he needed to know within twenty-four hours. But he wanted Clea to tell him what haunted her, why she was so adamant against any kind of commitment.

Usually he had very little interest in the motives of the women he dated.

His hotel had an exquisite stucco courtyard filled with exotic trees and flowering shrubs, leading into a neoclassical lobby with a marble floor on which Clea's heels tapped decisively. The restaurant overlooked the cliffs with their fur of vegetation, and the dark silky water. Hadn't Clea once compared his eyes to that enigmatic midnight-blue?

As they sat down, Slade said easily, "I've never really liked Monaco—tiers of buildings all the way down the slopes to the water's edge. No room to breathe."

"Where do you go to breathe, Slade?"

Her eyes were flickering down the menu. He let his gaze wander her features, rediscovering them with secret hunger: winged brows, delectably kissable lips, determined chin.

Sensing his scrutiny, Clea looked up; the expression in his eyes brought a wash of color to her cheeks. "You just have to look at me," she said in a strangled voice.

"And…?"

"Never you mind. Bad for your ego."

He threw back his head and laughed. "You make me feel as though I own the entire principality of Monaco."

"Casino and all?"

"The gamble paid off, didn't it? Here we are, having a meal together."

She bit her lip. "I didn't expect to see you in the bar tonight."

"Are you sure that's true?"

"Most men wouldn't have stayed." She gave him an unhappy smile. "I call it The Test. I figured you'd fail it."

He grinned. "That's what I figured you'd figure."

Feeling hunted, she burst out, "Why did you stay? The noise, the crowds, hours and hours with nothing to do but wait…you must have hated it."

"You and I are meant to be together. In bed. That's why I stayed."

Clea's knuckles on the leather-bound menu tightened with strain. "You say that as though it's an immutable truth."

"It is."

The clippings had always been her first line of defense, The Test her second. She had only one more weapon: this one had to work. "I told you I date lots of different men, Slade. Take it or leave it—because I won't change for you or for anyone else."

"So the battle lines are drawn," he said softly.

"If sailors have a girl in every port, I have a man in every major city in Europe." She slammed the menu shut. "I'll have a Salade Niçoise with tapenade."

The waiter materialized beside their table. "Madame? M'sieur?"

After Clea gave her order, Slade requested a bottle of wine by the number on the list, and for himself *daube,* wild boar simmered in red wine with herbs and garlic. Red meat, that's what he needed.

As though they hadn't been interrupted, he said, ticking off his fingers, "First, I'm not dating anyone else and I have no plans to do so—you're the one I want. Second, I've shown you tonight that I'm capable of hanging in. Of passing your ridiculous test." He allowed a little of his anger to surface. "When and where will our next date be? And this time it'll be a specific time on a specific day."

The waiter appeared with the bottle of wine Slade had ordered, a Burgundy from a château in the north of Burgogne. Clea glanced casually at the label. The color drained from her face; her gasp of dismay was audible. Puzzled, Slade said, "I should have consulted you—you don't like Burgundy? It's an excellent wine, I've had it before."

"No," she muttered, "it's fine. I—someone I know owns the vineyard, that's all."

She looked as though she could very easily burst into tears. The man who'd hurt her, was he the vintner? Another mystery, Slade thought, and went through the ritual of sniffing the cork and tasting the wine.

As warm, crusty baguettes were put on their table, Slade lifted his glass. "To the places where we can breathe."

She picked up her glass as if she were about to drink poison. "To freedom," she said, and for a moment looked as though her heart could break. Then she tossed back half the glass. Promptly the waiter refilled it.

Slade said easily, "My parents for as long as I can remember have owned a house on the coast of Maine. A rambling old place with a wide veranda facing the sea, its own private beach and acres of woodland. I've always loved it—the wind blows all the way from Portugal, and the air's so pure you can fill your lungs with salt and fog."

"You're very lucky," Clea said stiffly and took another gulp of wine.

Slade was drinking almost nothing. He wanted all his wits about him; he had no idea what was going on. Every time he saw her, wasn't he being drawn deeper and deeper into the mystery that was Clea?

"I was exceptionally lucky to have done a lot of my growing up in Maine," he said, telling her some of his escapades as a boy along the rocky shoreline, hoping she'd relax. The level of wine in the bottle sank steadily.

Their meals arrived. Clea looked down at her salad and the toast spread with olives, capers and anchovies; her appetite had vanished. As she picked up her fork, Slade said, "I'm unavailable for the next two weeks. A tour of some factories in Russia and Siberia that's taken the better part of six months to organize. But we could meet after that."

She swallowed some more wine. "On my terms," she said.

"For now," Slade said softly.

Implacable, she thought. Immovable. Irresistible. She should run away as far and as fast as she could. She said rapidly, gazing at her leafy green salad, "I'll be in Denmark the week after that. We can meet at Tivoli in Copenhagen—their annual Christmas market will be open."

"What are you doing in Denmark?"

That was her secret, one she had no intention of sharing with him. "Freedom means not having to account to anyone for the way you spend you time."

"Or does it mean—as the song says—that you've nothing left to lose?"

"You can't lose what you've never had. Pour me some more wine, Slade."

As he complied, he said evenly, "You said your grandfather left you his money—when did your parents die?"

An anchovy dropped from her fork. "If you meet me in Tivoli, do you plan to take me to bed?"

"Yeah," he said, "that's the plan."

"What if I say no?"

"I'll just have to change your mind, won't I?"

She said with the dignity of someone who'd drunk a half

a bottle of full-bodied Burgundy in a very short time, "Lust is overrated. That's all that's between us…the oldest instinct in the book. Once you got sex out of the way, you'd forget all about me. So what's in this for me?"

"How about the best sex you've ever had in your life?"

With an inner quiver of laughter that edged on hysteria, Clea knew she'd have almost nothing to compare it with. Another secret she wasn't going to share. She said haughtily, "You're much too sure of yourself."

Slade wasn't as sure of himself as he might have sounded: his gut was in a turmoil and the wild boar could have been hamburger. She was like quicksilver, he thought. Impossible to pin down. As for analyzing her in any rational way, forget it.

The waiter appeared and topped up Clea's glass. "Would m'sieur like to order a second bottle?"

Clea said, "M'sieur would not. Madame has drunk more than enough."

Not sure if he wanted to laugh or hit her on the head with the nearly empty wine bottle, Slade said tightly, "After we have sex in Copenhagen—because we're not talking about making love here—we go our separate ways…is that how you see it?"

"Once you have sex," she parried, "you lose interest. Right?"

She was, unfortunately, rather too close to the truth. "Who's the man who owns the vineyard, Clea? And what did he do to you?"

She put her glass down so fast that wine slopped over the rim onto the back of her hand. Red as blood, Slade thought, and saw that she was very lightly trembling. She said, "You could easily find out—we both know that."

"I could. But I'm not going to. You have a right to your privacy. Plus I'd much rather you told me yourself."

"As if that's going to happen."

"Bitterness doesn't become you."

"Not everyone has led your charmed life, Slade."

He thought of that dark, cold room, quiet as death. "I guess I've been luckier than most," he said noncommittally.

Her head jerked up. "I hit a nerve, didn't I?" she said evenly. "I'm sorry."

Taking his napkin, he wiped the wine from her hand, then covered her fingers with his own. The words that came out of him were totally unplanned. "Why do I get the impression you're the loneliest woman I've ever met?"

"Stop," Clea whispered, her hand curling into his in a way that touched him to the heart. "Or you'll have me crying like a baby."

"I have two shoulders and they're available anytime you want to cry on them," he said, and knew this simple offer felt unlike anything he'd ever said before. He'd never wanted women crying on his shoulder. Or on any other part of his anatomy.

She mumbled, "You make it sound so easy."

"Clea, I wish you'd tell me what's wrong."

"I can't. I never do." She tugged her hand free, and dabbed at the tears that were hanging on her lashes.

At least she wasn't denying that something was wrong. But what had the man who owned the vineyard done to her? And why did he, Slade, care?

He said, "Tivoli. Three weeks. When and where?"

"The first Saturday in December at five in the afternoon. There's only one patron saint for the season. Find him and you'll find me."

"I'll do that," Slade said. But by then, he thought, all her defenses would be firmly in place in again.

"Maybe you'll meet someone else in the meantime."

"Maybe the casino will go broke."

"You're right," she snorted, "I'm never bored with you. I want a piece of chocolate torte."

"After anchovies? You'll have nightmares."

"I don't dream," she said lightly. "Do you? What's your worst nightmare?"

He wasn't going to tell her about the underground room. So how could he fault her silence on the subject of the vintner? "That my mother will lose her recipe for smoked salmon fish-cakes with rhubarb chutney," he said promptly.

The conversation went from cooking to country inns, and from there to the winners of the Cannes Film Festival. Slade ordered a cab to take her to her hotel in Fontvieille. As they crossed the courtyard to wait for it, he noticed for the first time that there were two large birdcages against the far wall, each covered by a linen cloth. "They're probably songbirds," he said. "A barbarous practice to keep them in cages, I always think."

She couldn't agree more. "Why don't we set them free?"

"Great idea," Slade said with a grin.

Swiftly they walked over to the cages. But when Clea lifted the first cover, she saw that the bird in the cage was a parrot, its feathers a deep blue. The second cage held a lime-green parrot. Both were sleeping, heads tucked under their wings.

Slade said, "We can't set them free, Clea. It's November, they'd die."

"Yes," she whispered, "they'd die," and let the cloth drop to cover the cage. She felt unutterably sad.

His one desire to comfort her, Slade slid an arm around her shoulders. The contact, warm, unbearably intimate, brought Clea back to her senses; she pulled away, her face wiped clean of any emotion. "The cab'll be waiting," she said.

"Let it wait. What's up?"

"I'm tired, I drank too much wine and I want to be alone."

"I don't care how many men you date, you're alone too much. In a cage of your own devising."

"You have no idea what my life is like!"

"I've seen enough of you to make an educated guess."

White-faced with rage, desperate to get away from him, she seethed, "If you ever get tired of windmills, you can take up psychiatry." Then she whirled, hurrying alongside the ornamental pond with its filagreed fountain, and the bougainvillea tumbling down the stucco walls. At the gateway, as she came to a halt beside two imposing urns filled with pale canna lilies, Slade caught up with her. The taxi was waiting, its engine running.

He was in no mood for subtlety. Seizing her by the arm, he rasped, "You can't run away from me...you know that, and so do I."

"I can run as far and as fast as I choose."

"Just make sure you end up at Tivoli in three weeks."

In an incendiary mixture of rage and desire, Clea reached up, took his jaw in her two hands, her nails digging into his skin, and kissed him hard on the mouth. Then she pivoted, opened the back door of the cab and slipped into the seat.

Reckless laughter sparking his eyes, Slade grabbed the door handle, holding it open. "For me, the earth just moved. Did it for you, Clea?"

"Too much wine," she retorted, wishing it were the truth, and gave the name of her hotel to the taxi driver. "Goodbye, Slade."

"Self-deception's a dangerous game," he said. "See you in three weeks."

As he very gently shut the door, her features were a study in conflicting emotions. The taxi drove away, Slade watching until its lights disappeared around the corner.

The parrots, in the morning, would still be in their cages. But what of Clea? Where would she be?

CHAPTER FIVE

COPENHAGEN in early December was unexpectedly cold, with a couple of inches of fresh snow. Slade had just flown in from Latvia; so he was wearing a sheepskin coat and fur-lined boots as he walked under the brightly lit archway at the main entrance to the Tivoli Gardens, on Vesterbrogade. He felt as strung out as a seven-year-old on Christmas morning.

Clea had haunted his thoughts for the last three weeks.

Tivoli in winter was far from a mere ghost of its summer festivities. Directly in front of him was a huge restaurant, its Moorish façade outlined in gold, red and green. Everywhere he looked was extravagantly lit, music lilting through the chill air. The lake gleamed with a thin skim of ice; from fairy-tale cottages drifted the warm odors of pastries and hot coffee; the pagoda's elegant roofline dominated the roller coaster's long coils and the tall spire of Det Gyldne Tårn, the Golden Tower.

Now all he had to do was find jolly St. Nicholas. And Clea.

He was forty-five minutes early, so he had lots of time. Although he spoke virtually no Danish, the first person Slade asked for directions replied in impeccable English; so within ten minutes, he was standing to one side of an arcade that sheltered a herd of stuffed reindeer, sacks of toys and a red-clad St. Nicholas with a white beard and gold-rimmed glasses. He was attended by several pixies, little gold bells jingling on their red-and-green costumes. None of them was nearly tall enough to be Clea. A crowd of children surged around St. Nick's knees, their parents watching from the sidelines.

From behind a big red sleigh a woman emerged, her arms laden with packages. She handed them to a couple of the pixies, then bent to speak to a little girl near the back of the crowd. Another little girl grabbed her sleeve, and soon a cluster of children was laughing and chattering around her.

Slade stood very still in the dark shadow of the building. This was a side to Clea he hadn't yet seen, and wouldn't have suspected. She looked completely at ease. She looked, he thought, as though she loved children, this woman who couldn't abide the possibility of commitment.

One more layer to the enigma that was Clea.

Then she glanced at her watch and stood up. A small boy was seated on the saint's knee. She walked over and lifted him off, handing him back to his mother. St. Nick said something to her. She laughed, giving his beard a playful tug. Then she went back to her job of taking presents from the sleigh.

Under his red costume and ripple of white beard, St. Nick could be anyone. As, for instance, one of the players in her famous field.

Slade checked his own watch. It was five minutes to five, time he made an appearance. He walked into the arcade.

When Clea appeared from behind the sleigh, passing her pile of gifts to the pixies, he said clearly, "*Goddag,* Clea. And that's fifty percent of my entire stock of Danish."

Although Clea was expecting him, she gave a tiny start, as always disconcerted by his sheer presence, so laden with animal magnetism. Forcing a practised smile to her lips, she said, "*Hej,* Slade…so you came."

"Did you expect otherwise?"

"I didn't give it much thought," she said loftily.

"You're a very bad liar," he said, and looked her up and down, taking his time. She was wearing a long hunter-green cashmere coat, against which her hair flared like a torch. The hood was lined in velvet and edged with white faux fur; her mittens were fluffy white mohair, her boots polished black leather.

He stripped off his glove and rested his hand against her cheek; it was pink with cold. Clea said, sounding not quite as adamant as she should, "Don't even think of kissing me in front of all these children."

"Not the kind of kiss I have in mind."

Color mounted her cheeks. She could imagine that kiss all too vividly. With a rather overdone pout she said, "You have a one-track mind."

"How are you?" he said abruptly.

She widened her eyes innocently. "Getting my Christmas fix out of the way early...I'm fine."

So that was the way she planned to play it, he thought: on the surface, everything light and easy. But when had he ever backed down from a challenge?

"You look gorgeously, sexily and utterly beautiful," he said. "Am I the first man to tell you that today?"

"As a matter of fact, you are."

"St. Nick must be blind—have you known him long?"

Her lashes flickered. "Three years."

The question was out before he could censor it. "Have you slept with him?"

"Pixies and children have big ears," she snapped. "Let's walk for a while, I love looking at all the lights."

"Let's," he said agreeably. But once they were outside, Slade pulled her into the shadow of a giant evergreen, his kiss fueled by three weeks of sexual frustration and far too many erotic dreams.

Despite her best intentions, Clea grabbed the collar of his jacket and kissed him back, her tongue entwined with his, her teeth bruising his lip. And was lost.

Heat surged through Slade's body, heat and a depth of hunger that overwhelmed him with its demands. He wanted to haul her behind the tree and make love to her against the trunk. Make love until neither one of them could breathe, until they were saturated with the body's sensations…and all the while, he savored the dart and thrust of her tongue, the yielding sweetness of her mouth crushed to his.

His heart hammering in his chest, Slade wrenched his head back. "If we don't quit right now," he gasped, "we'll be flat on the ground underneath this tree."

Her rapid breathing made little puffs of white in the cold air. She said shakily, "That'd ruin my coat."

"We certainly deserve better than pine needles for a bed the first time we make love."

"We're not going to make love—ever!"

His heartbeat had settled to a steady throbbing. "You haven't answered my question yet."

"I forget what it was," she muttered.

"Jolly old St. Nicholas, was he a lover of yours?"

Patches of hectic color staining her cheeks, she said, "I don't keep asking you about your sexual history."

"You showed me the clippings, so I'm not expecting you to be a virgin—you're twenty-six years old, you come with a past. But I sure as hell don't want to be tripping over ex-lovers every step we take."

Wondering when she'd ever been so angry, Clea snapped, "I hear you, Slade. Put your voice one notch higher and all of Tivoli will hear you."

"Just so long as you do." Taking her by the hand, he led her away from the tree and deliberately changed the subject.

"I've just come from Latvia—I had to make a side trip there after Moscow. The weather was cold enough to encourage mass emigration to the Caribbean."

His profile, predatory as a hawk's, was etched against the lights. "What were you doing in Latvia?"

Being as entertaining as he knew how, Slade began describing some of the ups and downs of the last three weeks, and was rewarded by her delightful cascade of laughter. They wandered some of the boutiques of the market, where Clea suddenly stopped by a long table. She picked up a small pin, an enameled teddy bear with a charming grin. "I'm going to buy it for you," she said. "Not that you resemble a teddy bear."

"Not a chance," Slade said, pleased beyond measure by the simple gift.

She took out her credit card. "It'll remind you of Christmas in Tivoli."

"Do you seriously think I'll forget it?"

"Ja," she said. "Men have short memories." Frowning in concentration, she pinned the teddy bear to the collar of his shirt. Her fingers brushed his throat; she was standing very close to him, her perfume wafting to his nostrils, complex and seductive.

*Men have short memories...*how he hated it when she lumped him in with half the human race. He said casually, *"Tak*—my only other Danish word. I have something for you, I found them on Fifth Avenue."

He took a small box out of his pocket and passed it to her. Clea blinked at the name of the jeweller, tore off the silver ribbon and opened the box. Inside were gold earrings in the shape of birds with wide-spread wings.

"They're free," she said blankly. "The birds, that is. I don't mean the earrings didn't cost—"

"I know what you mean. That's why I bought them."

For a horrible moment Clea wondered if she was going to

burst into tears. She struggled to subdue them, smoothing her features into the mask she'd perfected over the years, and tucked the box into her black leather shoulder purse. "They're lovely, thank you."

Her defenses were a mile high, just as Slade had suspected they'd be. What, other than kissing her, could breach them? Wasn't that what he was here to find out? "Let's walk some more," he said.

They followed the circumference of the lake. On the far shore, a small group of teenagers came into sight, shoddily dressed, not as clean as they might have been. Clea stiffened, horrified; she had to get out of here before they recognized her. "Let's go this way, Slade," she said hastily, indicating another path and tugging at his sleeve. "We can get a better view of the roller coaster."

Going on instinct, he said, "We'll come back to the roller coaster in a minute—I'd like to take a look at that building up ahead."

"But—"

The girl in front, who had studs in her ears, nose and lower lip, cried out Clea's name, ran toward her and launched into a rapid stream of Danish. The other kids crowded around Clea, all of them obviously delighted to see her.

Who were they, Slade wondered, and what was their connection to Clea? Who, noticeably, was making no attempt to introduce them to him.

She was carrying it off, he thought, although beneath the banter she was exchanging with the kids, she looked thoroughly discomfited. Fiercely he wished he spoke Danish.

After a loud chorus of goodbyes and several sidelong glances at him, the teenagers kept going. Slade said casually, "What was that all about?"

"You couldn't follow?" Clea asked, keeping her voice casual with a huge effort. "You really don't speak Danish?"

"*Goddag* and *tak*—that's the extent of it."

She said with partial truth, "They panhandle by the station. I gave them money once and started talking to them, that's all."

"I don't think so," he said in a steel voice.

"Are you calling me a liar?"

"What's the rest of the story, Clea?"

"I liked them," she said. "I made long-term arrangements for them to sleep in a hostel at my expense." Which was also a partial truth. "Now can we please talk about something else?"

"That was kind of you," he said.

"With the amount of money I have? Scarcely."

"You got personally involved—that's what's kind. Anyone can give money away."

Belle, he thought, making a lightning-swift connection. Belle gets involved, too. Was that the root of the connection between Clea and Belle?

Mystery piled upon mystery. He said, "Let's find somewhere to eat."

"There's a very classy restaurant at my hotel," Clea said stiffly.

Seduction looked like the last thing on her mind and he wasn't formally dressed. "I saw a place near the concert hall," he said, and within five minutes they were seated in a folksy cottage whose menu was in both English and Danish. Once they'd dealt with the waiter, Slade said evenly, "You still haven't answered my question. So I'll answer it. I'd be willing to bet you haven't slept with St. Nick."

Clea looked at him warily. He was, of course, right. "Why do you say that?"

"Remember the clippings? The more I see of you, the less I'm inclined to believe that they're evidence of—what should I call it?—promiscuity? A very active love life?" He paused, struck as always by the intelligence in her gaze and the vulnerable curve of her mouth. "There's something about you," he went on slowly. "An almost untouched quality…"

Skewered to her seat by his dark eyes, Clea said in a brittle voice, "You can believe what you want to believe."

"Smoke screens—they're your specialty."

"You know the saying," she retorted, "no smoke without a fire."

"You didn't know what a fire was until you met me."

"How can you say that?" she flashed.

"I scared you witless the first time we kissed—on Fisherman's Wharf, remember?—because I got you in touch with the passionate woman you're meant to be. Who's a far cry from the woman in those clippings."

"You should be writing novels," she said sarcastically. "Fiction's definitely your specialty."

He said with growing conviction, "Nothing you could show me will persuade me you're shallow and flighty, changing men as easily as you change your shoes. It doesn't go with the Clea I'm starting to know. The one who wants to free caged parrots, who befriends a bunch of down-at-heel teenagers, who talks to little children as though they're real people." He took a deep breath. "I think that's the real woman."

"You're making this far too complicated!"

Was he? "You're a mass of contradictions. You sleep around, or so you're implying. Yet you won't let me near you. I—"

Someone was speaking to him in Danish. It was the waiter, holding out two platters of steamed mussels in apple cider broth. Slade raked his fingers through his hair. "*Tak,*" he said.

He felt frustrated, stirred up and confused. The one thing he didn't feel was hungry.

As the waiter vanished, Clea impulsively reached over and rested her hand on Slade's "This is what I was afraid of—that

I'd cause you pain," she said jaggedly. "It's why I did my best to send you away the very first time we met."

Her fingers were slender and ringless, her nails tinted a soft pink. He could see the tracery of blue veins under her smooth, ivory skin. As though he couldn't help himself, he lifted her hand to his mouth and closed his eyes, inhaling her scent, feeling her warmth lance through his own skin, intimate and desired. His pulse began to hammer; his groin hardened.

Was he being a fool to ignore the evidence she'd presented him with? Or was he simply being true to his deepest instincts?

When he looked up, Clea's gaze went straight through him, for it was blurred with desire and helpless longing. Tears hung on her lashes; her turquoise eyes were as vulnerable as he'd ever seen them. If a simple caress laid her so devastatingly open, how would the act of love affect her?

There was only one way to find out.

He said with iron implacability, "I'm not like the rest of your men—I won't jump at your whim, or conveniently disappear when you want me to. I'm different, you said so yourself. So why don't you try something different? Radically different. Exclusivity. With me."

She tugged her hand free and swiped at her eyes, knowing his caress had touched her in a place she strove to keep untouched. Inviolate. "Whenever I'm anywhere near you, I want so desperately to make love with you—even though you scare me half to death. But I don't do commitment, Slade. Not for anyone."

His gut churning, Slade said forcibly, "Spend Christmas with me and my family. Get to know me. Change your mind."

She picked up her fork and extracted a plump mussel from its shell. "I spend every Christmas with friends in Trinidad," she said repressively. "No St. Nick, no turkey dinner, no children, no snow."

"No family?"

"Definitely no family."

He remembered her lifting the little boy, the way the child had laughed down at her. "Don't you want children of your own?"

She flinched. "Perhaps. Someday."

"Then you're going to have to make a commitment, aren't you?" he said, and saw that, for once, she had no glib reply, no clever retort.

He began to eat, noticing that tonight she was scarcely touching her wine. He was the one who felt like getting drunk, he thought wryly. Had he ever met a woman as stubborn as Clea Chardin? As determined to avoid anything that remotely smacked of exclusivity? Usually it was the other way around, women latching on to him with wedding bells ringing in their ears.

Poetic justice, that's what his father would call it.

"There's a lot of garlic in these mussels," he said easily. "Good thing we're both eating them."

"Don't assume you'll be kissing me again."

"It's not an assumption—it's a certainty."

Her eyes flitted down to her plate. "We'll see about that," she said, and determinedly led the conversation into the murky field of Russian politics.

It was a conversation Slade was quite capable of sustaining. After they'd finished eating, they took a cab to her hotel, Clea sitting as far from him on the seat as she could.

In an elegant enclave of eighteenth century rococo buildings, the cab drew up in front of a stone hotel named after Den Lille Havfrue, the Little Mermaid. "She was the daughter of the sea king, who lost herself when she fell in love with a human," Clea said, a slight edge to her voice. Then panic tightened all her nerves as she saw Slade reach for his wallet. "You don't need to get out," she added jerkily.

"I'll see you indoors," he said, and paid off the cabbie.

Clea didn't want Slade accompanying her into the hotel: not when her own body was so intent on betraying her. "The name of the hotel is one reason I stay here," she gabbled. "Plus it's wonderfully comfortable, and small enough to be friendly without being intrusive. I love strolling around Frederiksstaden, all the palaces and the cobbled square—the guards look so solemn in their blue trousers and fur hats."

Clea wasn't a woman to make small talk; she was nervous, Slade thought, and covering it with chatter. The doorman in his deep plum coat ushered them into the lobby, where gilded columns surrounded an antique table crowned with a huge bouquet of lilies.

Clea turned to face Slade, her voice higher-pitched than usual. "Good night."

He said curtly, "We haven't made any arrangements for our next date. And we're not going to do that in a public place. What floor's your room on?"

She could throw a tantrum, or she could scream for help: either of which would ruin her reputation here forever. She said helplessly, "My suite's on the top floor."

The elevator smoothly whisked them up five floors, depositing them on a thick floral carpet outside four tall, gilt-engraved doors. Clea chose the one on the left and inserted her card. The door opened with a click. She walked in, throwing back her hood and tossing her coat on a velvet-upholstered chaise longue. Swiftly Slade surveyed his surroundings. More rococo elegance; the bedroom door was wide-open. Through it, he could see the wide bed, canopied and draped in plum brocade.

His heartbeat quickened. He brought his gaze back to Clea. Her dress was black, severely cut, yet all the more provocative for the way it skimmed her hips, and gently outlined the swell of her breasts. Awkwardly she kicked off her boots, her high-arched feet and slender legs exquisite in black hose.

Beneath a thin veneer of composure, she now looked outright terrified.

A cold fist clenched around his heart. How could he seduce her when she looked like a wild creature at bay? "Clea, I don't force women," he said flatly, "it's not my style. You'll come willingly to my bed or not at all. So there's no need for you to look so frightened."

"It's myself I'm frightened of," she said wretchedly. "I thought you knew that."

With a tiny sound of compassion, Slade took her in his arms. She held herself rigidly; at the base of her throat the pulse fluttered under her skin. He smoothed her hair with one hand, tipped her chin and kissed her gently on the mouth.

Had he ever kissed a woman with this overwhelming need to comfort her?

Her body gradually relaxed, her lips soft and warm, opening to him. With all the control he could muster, Slade moved back, and knew he'd never done anything more difficult.

"Florence," he said. "In ten days. My house there is small, but it has central heating."

Aching for the touch of his mouth, Clea gaped at him. "Florence?" she croaked. "Our next date?"

"Yeah…do me a favor, will you? Don't date anyone else in the interim."

Almost, she weakened. She'd felt safe in his arms, she thought unhappily. Protected. Yet nothing in her experience encouraged her to trust either feeling. "You're putting me in a cage, Slade. Like the parrots."

"If that's what you truly believe, then you're in trouble."

She said, despair flattening her voice, "If we keep on

seeing each other, we'll get involved more and more deeply."

"That's right," Slade said inflexibly. "I'll give you my address in Florence and I'll meet you at the airport."

"You wear me down," she muttered, then heard her own words replay in her head. She sounded defeated. Beaten. Like the coward he'd accused her of being.

She could handle Slade Carruthers, she decided in a flare of defiance; certainly she could be every bit as stubborn as he. "I love Florence," she said steadily, "I always have."

"Along with New York, it's my favorite city in the world."

"I'm not responsible if you get hurt, Slade."

"We're all responsible for the consequences of our actions."

"There's a costume museum one street north of Ponte Vecchio," she said rapidly. "I'll meet you there. Three in the afternoon on the sixteenth."

"Do you promise there'll be no one else between now and then?"

"If you're talking sex, it's highly unlikely in the next ten days," she said, her cheeks flaming. "But I have two dinner dates I'm not going to cancel—I won't have restrictions put on what I do."

Forgetting all his good intentions, Slade stepped closer to her, pulled her the length of his body and kissed her parted lips with ferocious hunger; she responded instantly and with a fervor that set his pulses racing. His hand found the sweet rise of her breast, where her nipple was tight as a bud; she moaned deep in her throat as he drew her hips into the hardness of his erection.

If he didn't stop now, he'd be lost.

On his terms. Hold that thought, Slade. Pushing her away, he said with assumed calm, "Then I'll say good night."

Her whole body on fire with needs she'd never known she possessed, Clea faltered, "You—you're not staying?"

"That's right."

"Why did you kiss me, then?" she demanded, her eyes blazing. "Leading me on this way?"

"Would you rather we'd had this discussion in the lobby?"

She wrapped her arms around her chest. "I'd rather you'd stayed in the cab," she said bitterly.

"I hoped, when we actually got within the vicinity of a bed, that you'd tell me you wouldn't date anyone else for the space of ten days," he said with matching anger. "It doesn't seem too much to ask."

"It's not the ten days—it's the principle of the thing!"

"Or," he rapped, "from my point of view, the lack of principle."

"So Florence is off," she said in an unreadable voice.

"Florence is very much on."

"What's that saying? A sucker for punishment—that's you, Slade."

"Have you ever heard of New England cussedness? It's another way of saying obstinate as a stone wall. That's me, Clea."

"The unbendable force meets the immovable object," she said softly. "That's us, Slade."

He tweaked a strand of her hair. "You got it, babe. See you in ten days at the museum. Sleep well—and if you dream, make sure it's about me."

Her eyes were brimming with a turmoil of fury and frustration. Desperate to get away from her, because if he didn't he'd end up in her bed despite all his fine pronouncements, Slade marched across the carpet to the door and let himself out. It closed with the same decisive click with which it had opened. He ran down the stairs and out into the cold night. Alone.

He was, he was sure, the very first man who, with the prospect of a night in Clea Chardin's delectable arms, had walked away from her.

More fool he.

CHAPTER SIX

SLADE walked down Via De'Benci toward the Arno. The light was golden and the sky a cloudless blue. There were few places he'd rather be than Florence on a sunny afternoon in December; especially when he'd be seeing Clea in a few minutes.

He dove into the network of streets that led him ever closer to the river, toward the famous Ponte Vecchio and the much less famous costume museum. He must ask Clea why, of all the illustrious museums in the city, she'd chosen that one.

He was going to make love to her this evening; he was tired of waking in the night and reaching for her, his body one big knot of frustration. Enough was enough. Besides, if he took her to bed, he was sure to break down some of the barriers she hid behind, even change her mind on the subject of fidelity.

The museum boasted Romanesque arches with Corinthian capitals, its stone frontage flanked by two fountains. The enormous oak door creaked as Slade pushed it open. The lobby was cool and high-ceilinged, peopled with astonishingly lifelike mannequins wearing everything from polished armor to the diaphanous robes Botticelli had immortalized.

The receptionist had classic Tuscan features and a warm smile. Slade paid the fee on his VISA; as she noted the name on his card, her lashes flickered in a way he was later to remember. Keeping his eyes open for Clea, he meandered from room to room, hard-pressed to resist such a beguiling tour of Florence's history.

Visitors with guidebooks and art students with easels were wandering around, but there was no sign of the woman he was looking for. In the last room his gaze flicked over the mannequins, a cold lump settling in his belly. She wasn't here. Had she given in to her fears and stayed away? Or had she been delayed in one of Florence's ubiquitous traffic jams?

He'd go back to the lobby and wait for her there. She'd turn up.

As he turned to leave, his gaze brushed over the figure of a woman standing on a pedestal. Her eyes gleamed in a way that was almost lifelike, he thought idly, and turned away. His steps faltered imperceptibly. Almost? They *were* lifelike. The woman's face was Clea's.

She'd moved slightly; that's why he'd noticed her in the first place.

With a superhuman effort Slade kept going, until he was hidden from her by one of the foot-thick walls. He leaned against it, wanting to laugh his head off. He had his answer: he now knew why she'd chosen this museum. Once again, she was testing him. With, he thought, her sense of humor very much to the fore.

Why wait for him by the front door like any other tourist? Much too boring and predictable a course of action for Clea. Wasn't her sense of fun one of the several reasons he was pulled so strongly toward her?

Two could play that game.

Approaching one of the art students, he said in Italian, "Would you do me a favor, you and your friends? Would you spend a few minutes sketching one of the costumes in the next room? The woman in the long green dress…I'd make it worth your while."

The students, all of whom looked like they could do with a square meal, talked in rapid-fire Italian for a couple of minutes. Then the bearded young man, who appeared to be their leader, pocketed the sheaf of bills Slade had produced. "*Si, si…grazie.*"

They picked up their gear and went into the next room. A few moments later Slade followed them. Clea was still stationed on the pedestal, her gaze demurely downcast. Her gown cupped her breasts, falling in long folds down her body; her starched white wimple completely covered her hair.

He said, a little too loudly, to the nearest of the students, "How fashions change. That woman wouldn't be called particularly beautiful today…yet in her time, she was probably considered a fine catch."

Clea's mouth twitched. He went on, "A pious and dutiful wife…her head full of heaven and the blandishments of her latest lover. And a mouth full of bad teeth."

"Unwashed, too," said the bearded young man, whose shirt was far from clean.

"Lice in her hair?" Slade suggested. "Not exactly a turn-on…I'll be back in a few minutes—I'm supposed to meet someone here, and she's late."

He walked away. But in ten minutes, judging that was long enough to have made Clea suffer, he was back. For a moment he stood in the doorway, looking at the scene with private pleasure. The setting sun was slanting through one of the high windows, dust motes floating gently downward on the silent collection of medieval knights and their ladies. The women's costumes glowed like jewels.

But Clea's face, he saw with sudden dismay, was ashen-pale. As he stepped out of the shadows into the light, she swayed on her feet, her eyes glassy.

He thrust through the group of students and leaped onto the platform on which her pedestal stood. As her head fell forward and her body slumped, he caught her in his arms.

Her forehead bumped his shoulder; she was as limp as a rag doll. Cursing himself for making her pose too long, Slade lowered her to the edge of the platform and pushed her head between her knees. Kneeling beside her, he said with a gentleness new to him, "Take your time—you fainted."

She made a tiny sound of distress. "Slade?" she whispered. "Is it you?"

"Yes, I'm here…I'm not going away."

"I…the room suddenly started to sway and I couldn't make it stop."

"It was my fault," he said harshly, "I shouldn't have left you standing so long."

She was pushing against him. "I need to lie down."

He put an arm under her knees and another around her back, lifting her in a single smooth movement. "I'll get a limo right away." He glanced over at the bearded student. "*Grazie.*"

"Slade, put me down!"

"No," he said. "I feel like a louse, and you must let me make amends."

He carried her through the series of rooms, ignoring the curious stares of the other visitors. In the lobby he asked the receptionist to call the limousine driver he always hired in Florence, whose station wasn't far from Ponte Vecchio. "Tell him to hurry," Slade said.

Quickly she did as he'd asked. Then she said, "The signora, is she all right?"

"She fainted…the rooms are very warm." He added, almost certain he was right, "You know her?"

"She's one of our best benefactors."

"Maddalena, be quiet," Clea gasped.

Maddalena went on, "This is, of course, why the signora is permitted to wear one of our gowns."

"We'll return it first thing tomorrow," Slade promised.

"That will be fine."

"I'll take good care of the gown, Maddalena," Clea said faintly. "Could you get my case?"

"Of course." The receptionist took a small black leather case from the cupboard behind her. "The signora's clothes," she said, handing it to Slade.

Five minutes later, Slade was easing Clea into the backseat of a sleek black limo. "*Buon giorno*, Lorenzo," he said. "Thanks for coming so quickly. Take me home, would you?"

Clea pushed herself upright against the seat, striving to gain some control over a situation that had the potential to thoroughly mortify her. "Slade, I want to go to my hotel."

"For once you're not getting your own way."

"Please—I just need to be alone for a while."

"Relax, we'll be at my place in ten minutes."

With something near despair she said, "I can't fight you—I don't have the energy."

"Then don't try," he said, smiling at her to take the sting out of his words. "Let someone else take charge of your life for a change."

If only it were that simple. If only her impulse to have a little fun in the museum hadn't backfired so badly. Clea leaned back, closing her eyes.

It was nearer twenty minutes before the limo drew up in front of an old stone house in the artisans' quarter. The cobbled street was narrow, the houses seeming to lean into one another, their walls illumined reddish gold as the sun sank further to the west. The limo driver got out and took the key Slade had passed him, unlocking an old oak door nestled in a masonry arch.

Slade smiled his thanks, lifted Clea as carefully as if she were breakable, and carried her inside; she was still pale, bluish shadows under her eyes. As the door closed behind them, he snagged the double latch and quickly disarmed the alarm system. The steps were wide, carpeted in rich burgundy; frescoes in earthy browns and reds adorned the plaster walls. He said easily, "I use the two bottom floors for business meetings, and keep my personal stuff on the top three floors."

His bedroom was on the very top floor, its little balcony with a view of the splendid gold-tipped spire on the Duomo and the faraway, misty outline of the Tuscan hills; it was a view he never tired of. His few treasures were set into alcoves in the wall: a small Donatello, an inlaid box that had belonged to one of the Medicis, a Verrocchio bronze of a young hunter. The bed was large, the wood with the patina of age, the spread the same faded red of the tile roofs of the city he so loved. Nothing matched in the room; yet it made a harmonious whole.

He put Clea down on the bed. She said, trying to push herself upright, "I wish you'd taken me back to my hotel."

Standing beside the bed, he said, "Let me look after you for once, Clea—independence is all very well, but it can be carried too far. And, to put it bluntly, you look awful."

"I never let anyone look after me," she said with a spurt of her normal spirit.

"We should all be open to new experiences," he said dryly. "Do you think I make a practice of looking after women?" Going over to the tall walnut wardrobe that took up the better part of one wall, he took out a shirt. "You can wear this. The first thing is to get that headdress off—it looks tight enough to make anyone faint."

"I can manage."

"I'm sure you can. But you're not going to."

He found the snaps at her nape, under the gauzy white

folds, and carefully removed the wimple, laying it on an old oak chest under the window. Then he reached for the buttons on the back of her gown.

In a strangled voice, knowing she couldn't postpone it any longer, Clea said, "I—I have to ask you to go to the *farmacia* for me—the drugstore."

"I've got a first-aid kit—what do you need? Something for a headache? A muscle relaxant?"

She wasn't wearing a bra; the long line of her spine filled Slade with a desperate longing to run his finger along the small bumps of her vertebrae. He eased the gown from her shoulders, picked up the shirt and slipped it around her.

She clutched the shirt to her breast as the gown fell to her waist. "You wouldn't have what I need," she muttered. "Or maybe you do and I'll hate you for it."

She was talking in riddles. "Stand up," he said, "and let's get rid of the gown. I'll get you something to warm your feet once you're in bed, then I'll find whatever it is you need."

"I'm early," she blurted, her eyes downcast, "that's why I'm not prepared. I'd never have done this silly skit with the gown if I'd realized…wrong time of the month, Slade. My period."

"Do you faint every month?" he said, appalled.

"No…but I don't stand on a pedestal trying to emulate a statue every month, either. I get cramps and I feel horrible for about twelve hours, that's all."

It sounded like more than enough to Slade. "Then I'm doubly glad you're here so I can look after you, and doubly sorry about the art students," he said. "Once you're settled, I'll go to the drugstore, there's one four streets over from here. Because no, I don't have what you need."

I'll hate you for it…did that mean she was jealous of any other women in his life?

She frowned at him. "This isn't what you'd planned for the evening."

As he helped her to her feet, the gown slithered to the floor. Clea automatically stepped out of it, kicking off delicate gold shoes at the same time. Slade said, "Roll with the punches. Always been one of my mottoes."

He pulled back the covers and eased her onto thin cotton sheets that smelled sweetly of lavender. "Lie down and stay down," he ordered. "Do you want something hot to drink? Herbal tea, perhaps?"

"I—no," she said clumsily. "But it was nice of you to ask." In a gesture that tore him to the heart, she snuggled into the pillow. "That feels better," she sighed. "Maybe you could bring me a muscle relaxant for the cramps."

Slade hung her gown in the wardrobe before running downstairs, where he found the vial of pills and poured some water into a crystal goblet. He'd bought a dozen pale yellow roses for the dining room table; picking them up, he carried them upstairs, too.

Clea was nearly asleep. "They're lovely," she mumbled. "My favorite color, how did you know?"

"I didn't. Happens to be my favorite, too."

"So we're meant for each other?" she said with a weak grin.

"Who knows?" Slade said soberly. He passed her the water along with the pill, propping her up as she took it. Warmth from her skin seeped through the shirt she was wearing. He said with a wry smile, "So here you are in my bed, Clea. Although not quite the way I'd imagined it."

She sank back on the pillows. "I must look about as seductive as a mud hen."

"You'd look seductive in a garbage bag. Are you warm enough?"

"Wonderfully warm," she said drowsily.

He wrote down his cell phone number. "The phone's here by the bed. Call me if you need anything more. I'll be back in fifteen minutes."

"Thanks," she murmured and closed her eyes.

He was still wearing his jacket over a Guernsey sweater. On the street he threaded through the people getting off work, his mind very much on Clea. If she'd had her way, she'd be back in her hotel right now, and he'd be a million miles away.

The thought of her in his bed filled him with an unsettling and poignant emotion he couldn't call by name. What was happening to him? She'd looked so fragile, so vulnerable, that his sole urge had been to look after her.

A whole new experience.

The drugstore was crowded. Slade stood in front of the dismayingly large array of neatly arranged boxes, knowing this was another new experience. Grabbing three different kinds, he marched toward the counter, paid for them and chastised himself for cowardice because he was relieved when the cashier put them in a brown paper bag.

Give him ten angry CEOs any day of the week.

Within twenty minutes he was climbing the stairs to his bedroom. When he walked in, Clea was asleep. She was lying on her back, her face turned sideways to the pillow. Her hair seemed to have drained her cheeks of all color; her eyes still had bruised shadows beneath them.

He left the package beside the bed and drew the curtains over the two narrow windows. Then he walked downstairs to the kitchen. They wouldn't be eating out tonight. So the meal was up to him.

Ribollita, he thought, with crostini spread with olive oil, wild mushrooms and chopped tomatoes. He had two helpings of outrageously expensive tiramisu from his favorite delicatessen, and if Clea liked to finish a meal with espresso, he always had that on hand.

After opening a bottle of red wine made from the Sangiovese grape of the Tuscan hills, he rolled up his sleeves and started making the rich vegetable soup, turning on one of the local radio stations to hear the news.

Sometime later, when the kitchen was redolent of herbs and garlic, Slade suddenly became aware he was being watched. He swiveled. Clea was leaning against the doorpost, his shirt falling to her thighs, her face delicately flushed. She said, "The apron becomes you."

He smiled. "I'm a messy cook. How are you feeling?"

"Better. Slade, I should go back to my hotel, you—"

"Supper's nearly ready. Would you like it in bed?"

"No! I—"

"Let me find you some sweatpants and a top, then we'll eat."

She looked around at the vegetable peelings on the butcher block, the crushed herbs and the bottle of thick tomato paste. "You cooked. For me," she said blankly.

"Yeah…" He put a little of the broth in a ladle and walked over to her. "Careful, it's hot. Enough salt, do you think?"

She sipped it gingerly. "It tastes heavenly."

"You don't have to sound so surprised."

She said stiffly, "I'm not used to a man who can make *ribollita* as though he was born here."

"I told you I was different," he remarked. "Let's eat in the kitchen."

The kitchen walls were sponged a soft blue, with terracotta accents. Herbs hung in bunches from the ceiling, while geraniums bloomed in bursts of red against the squared windowpanes. The table and chairs had come from an old Tuscan farmhouse; Slade had lovingly polished them until they shone.

"It's charming," Clea said, wondering if Slade would ever stop surprising her.

He pulled out one of the chairs. "Sit, Clea. I'll bring something for you to wear."

"This place," she said in a rush, "it's like a real home."

She looked strained and unhappy. Not bothering to disguise his compassion, he said, "Where's your real home?"

"I don't have one."

"We all need a place we can call home."

She should never have revealed her lack of a home to a man as acute as Slade. "I'm hungry, Slade. Feed me."

"Sure I will," he said. "But we're not done with this conversation."

He took the stairs two at a time, grabbed some clothes from the wardrobe and went back to the kitchen. She had to roll the waistband of his sweatpants several times to get them to stay up, even with the help of his Gucci belt; the cuffs of his sweater swallowed her fingertips. He said, "Armani wouldn't hire you for the catwalk."

She gave a snort of laughter, tightening the belt. "I wouldn't be seen dead on Via de'Tornabuoni right now."

He served her a bowl of soup, putting the crostini on the table, and pouring her a glass of wine. Then he lit the beeswax candles in a battered silver candelabra that had come from a fifteenth century Benedictine abbey. Sitting down across from her, he raised his glass. "May you find your true home, Clea."

She sent a hunted glance around the kitchen. "This is all so domesticated."

"Domesticated, from *domus*. Which means home."

"I'm not used to it, that's all I meant."

"I know what you meant."

She took a big bite of toast slathered with wild mushrooms. "Mmm…delicious. Do you cook like this all the time?"

"Mostly when I'm here. I get tired of fancy restaurants—don't you?"

She closed her eyes in bliss as she savored a mouthful of the broth. "I've never thought about it."

"Time you did."

She didn't want to. "Who does the dishes?" she asked.

"I do. With the help of the most modern of dishwashers that I keep hidden in the pantry so it won't wreck the decor."

"No servants?"

"Caretakers live in the flat behind the house. Cleaners come every week. But when I'm here I like the place to myself." He cut her a chunk of cheese. "I spend a lot of time with people, most of whom want something from me. Or whose minds I'm trying to pry away from instant profits to long-term considerations—like an environment that'll be fit for their grandchildren. So here I prefer my own company."

"And the company of women."

"Not here," he said.

Her spoon halted halfway to her mouth. "You must bring your women here—why wouldn't you?"

"I told you—this is my retreat." He leaned forward. "You're the first woman to be in that bed."

The spoon sloshed back into her soup. "I don't believe you!"

"You'd better. Because it's true."

Something in his face finally convinced her. She said uneasily, "Why did you bring me here then?"

"The alternative was to abandon you in a hotel," he said. "Be damned if I was going to do that. Eat your soup. You wouldn't want to insult the cook—he's bigger than you are."

Her eyes narrowed. "It's a measure of the excellence of the soup that I'm doing what I'm told."

"I'm flattered," Slade said, and asked her what other museums she frequented in Florence. From there, the conversation ranged easily over many subjects, until finally he was pouring espresso into tiny pottery mugs.

Then Clea said, feeling like a dog worrying a bone, "This house—it must have cost a fortune."

"Several, when you include furniture, taxes and upkeep."

"I don't understand how you've made it into a home…"

"It's because I love it. And everything in it."

Restlessly she wriggled her shoulders. "I'm a hotel person—here one day and gone the next. No attachments. Nothing to hold me down."

"Then, in my opinion, you're the loser. This place is real, Clea. Real and lasting and loved."

She was glaring at him as though he was an enemy. "I don't get it."

"Get what?"

Sweeping her arm to encompass the messy kitchen, she said choppily, "You put me to bed, you went to the *farmacia* for me, you cooked for me—what's in it for you, Slade?"

"I did it because I wanted to."

"There's no payoff—we both know that."

Anger uncoiled within him. "You mean sexual payoff?"

"Of course."

"What kind of men do you date?" he exploded.

"The kind who'd have put me in a taxi and sent me back to my hotel. Alone. Which is what I wanted you to do."

"How many times do I have to tell you I'm different from the rest?"

She said with icy precision, "What was the real reason you didn't you go to bed with me in Copenhagen?"

"I told you—I'm not going to tumble in and out of bed with you while you date men from every corner of Europe. Both of us deserve better than that. You'll commit yourself to me for the duration of our affair—or there won't be one."

She pounced. "And which one of us decides when the affair is over?"

He didn't have a clue. "We can argue about that later," he said, knowing it for a weak reply.

She pushed back her chair, wood scraping on the ceramic tile. "I really hate this conversation."

"Because I'm not jumping to your tune like the rest of your men?"

"Because sooner or later you'll dump me like you've dumped all your other women. So I'm dumping you first. Right now."

"Sure—run away. You're good at that."

"Yes," she said, "I am. It's called self-preservation."

She stood up. She should have looked ridiculous in her borrowed clothes; instead she looked beleaguered, defiant and very unhappy. Slade got to his feet, too. With raw honesty he said, "I'm offering you the best gifts of my body, Clea. I'll be as good to you as I know how, give you all the pleasure I'm capable of. But I'm not offering marriage, and I won't share you with anyone else."

The best gifts of my body...

A wave of flame swept over her; for a crazy moment she wondered if she was going to faint again. "I'm going upstairs to change," she said jaggedly, "then I'll get a cab to my hotel."

She walked past him, hitching at his Gucci belt, the shoulder seams of his sweater halfway to her elbows. Slade stood still, breathing hard. He'd give her five minutes. Then he was going after her.

After pouring the last of the soup into a plastic container, he loaded the dishwasher and left the kitchen, taking the stairs two at a time. Outside his bedroom door he paused for a minute to gather his wits; and with a jolt realized he could see Clea in the reflection from his mirror. She was standing by the bed in a chocolate-brown suit, the skirt several inches above the knee, the jacket smoothly skimming her body. She was holding his sweater to her face, her nose buried in it, her eyes closed.

Then, in a gesture of shocking suddenness, she flung the sweater on the bed and bent to put on her shoes.

Slade walked into the room.

CHAPTER SEVEN

"I'M NEARLY ready to call the cab," Clea said tightly. "And don't you dare blame this whole mess on hormones."

"I wasn't about to blame it on anything but sheer cussedness—you'd make a fine New Englander." Slade took her by the elbows and spoke from somewhere deep inside him. "You're as white as the sheets on the bed—stay here, Clea, sleep in the bed, and I'll sleep in the guest room."

"Stop treating me as though I'll break—this happens every month," she said irritably. "And the answer's no."

"Then you're still being a coward."

She broke free, marched over to the bureau and picked up a silver-framed photo, waving it wildly in the air. "These are your parents, aren't they?"

He'd taken the snapshot of David and Bethanne on the verandah of their house in Maine, the sea a sparkling backdrop; both his parents looked happy and relaxed. "That's right."

"If their marriage is so great, why are you still a bachelor? You're a decent man, don't think I can't see that—put decency together with a whole lot of money and that sexy cleft in your chin, and the women must mob you. Yet here you are, having one carefully orchestrated affair after another."

"I've never met a woman who tempted me to change that pattern."

"So you expect me to fall into it."

"You know what? I bet none of the rest of your men has ever made you lose control—made you so desperate for love-making that you can't sleep or eat. Tell me I'm wrong."

How could she, when it would be a blatant lie? "None of them frighten me, either," she retorted.

"You can't spend the rest of your life scared of your own shadow," Slade said forcefully.

He'd had more than enough of words. Taking her in his arms, he began kissing her, enveloped in a hunger that threatened to devour him. His hands ranged her back, buried themselves in her tangled curls, cupped the sweet curve of her breast and soft rise of her hip. And all the while his lips feasted on her, his tongue dancing with hers.

Knowing she couldn't help herself, Clea kissed him back, her fingers tugging at the buttons on his shirt, slipping beneath the fabric to trace the arc of bone and heat of muscle. Was this home? she thought in true confusion. The only home she'd ever known?

As she rubbed against him, inflaming him beyond any control, Slade muttered, "Stay with me, Clea. I don't care if we can't make love—let me at least hold you, have you in my bed where you belong."

"You make the bones melt in my body," she whispered. "I want you as I've never wanted a man before…you're right, that's what I can't deal with—how I'm so out of control."

He slid his mouth down the entrancing tautness of her throat, finding the little pulse at its base, feeling through every nerve the frantic racing of her blood. "We're not going to make love," he said huskily. "So you're safe to stay."

"And what about next time? What do we do then?"

"Let's take one day at a time."

Her eyes held all the turmoil of the ocean. "You'll still want to make love to me, and—"

"Sure I will. But only if you promise that we'll stop chasing each other all over Europe, and that you won't date anyone else. As for me, I swear I won't dump you between one night and the next, as if you're disposable. As if you have no feelings. Do you think I can't see how vulnerable you are?"

Trembling very lightly, on the verge of tears, she cried, "You terrify me, Slade. If we had an affair, you'd turn my life upside down, and then you'd leave me with nothing. I can't do that. We mustn't see each anymore, it's too painful, it tears me apart."

Pulling free, Clea picked up the phone by the bed, punched in some numbers and spoke in rapid Italian. Banging the receiver back into its cradle, she announced, "A cab'll be here in five minutes—I have a regular driver when I'm in Florence."

Then she grabbed her long gown, her wimple and gold slippers and her black case. Head high, she marched out of the bedroom.

Slade stood still. The sheets were crumpled from Clea's body. His parents smiled at him from the bureau. The thick curtains masked any view of the city he loved.

Raking his fingers through his hair, he started down the stairs, his steps muffled by the thick carpet. Clea was standing at the bottom by the big oak door, leaning against the wall, her eyes shut. She looked frighteningly fragile. He said harshly, "You leaving like this, it's all wrong."

"For me to stay would be wrong."

"Running away is what's wrong. I don't have a clue who hurt you so badly, although I'd sure like to punch the bastard into the middle of next week. But you can't hide from him all your life—because then he's running the show."

"You don't understand!"

"Then explain it to me so I can. Tell me about him—that way, there'll be no risk of a repeat."

She shook her head, her hair falling forward to hide her

face. Inside Slade, anger defeated compassion. He was living in the wrong century, he thought savagely. If he were a Medici, he wouldn't be standing here like a block of wood letting the woman he desired walk out the door. "No matter where you run, I can always track you down," he said in a voice that he scarcely recognized as his own.

"If you have any feelings for me at all, you won't do that," Clea said, her turquoise eyes full of pleading. "I—the taxi should be here by now."

As she tugged the door open, a white cab pulled up and blasted its horn. "Goodbye, Slade. Take care of yourself," she muttered. Then, clutching her clothes, she dived into the backseat of the taxi, and it drove away.

Slade closed the door. The thick walls of his house deadened most of the street noise; had he ever felt so utterly alone?

Grabbing his jacket from the hook, he went outdoors, into the bustle and confusion of one of Florence's narrow alleys. The taxi had disappeared.

The shops of the artisans and restoration workers, the ice cream parlour near Santa Croce, the crenellated twelfth century tower of the Bargello where executions had run rampant, Slade strode past them all, hardly seeing them. Even the magnificent Piazza del Duomo for once failed to move him.

He headed back toward the Arno, into the western quarter of the city, marching along street after street until it was well past midnight. The smell of roasted chestnuts died away as the vendors went home. The traffic lessened. And still he walked.

He'd let her get away: the only woman who'd ever touched him in depths he hadn't known were his.

At seven-thirty the next morning, Slade was dreaming. Hands and ankles in chains, his elbows gripped by two armored guards, he was being led toward a scaffold in the arched courtyard of the Bargello. Somewhere high above his head a bell tolled, once, twice, heavy with doom.

Sweating, his heart pounding, he sat up in bed. A bell was ringing. The telephone.

He picked up the receiver and said hoarsely, "Carruthers."

"Slade?"

He cleared his throat. "Clea?" he said stupidly.

"Are you all right? You sound terrible."

"I was asleep. Where are you?"

"I'm at the airport and—"

All his anger surged to the surface. "Of course you're at the airport. That's what you do best, isn't it? Here one day and gone the next. Believe me, I—"

"Will you please shut up and listen! I want you to meet me in Paris. On Tuesday. For dinner at La Marguerite, do you know it?"

"Everyone knows it. Best restaurant in Paris. The answer's no."

"Look, I know I didn't handle last night very well and I'm sorry. I'm not playing games, really I'm not. There's someone I want you to meet," she said, her words tumbling over each other. "He usually eats at La Marguerite on Tuesdays. It'd help you to understand why I'm the way I am—that's why I'm suggesting it."

Slade rubbed his eyes, trying with all his willpower to fight off the dread and foreboding of his dream. "All right," he said curtly. "What time?"

"Eight-thirty. I'll look after the reservation…thank you, Slade." There was a small pause, during which he could hear a loudspeaker announcing the next flight. She said in a rush, "I've got to go, they're calling my flight. I'll see you on Tuesday."

The connection was cut. Slade put down the phone and got out of bed. Pulling back the curtains, he looked out over the ranked rooftops of Florence, and belatedly his brain began to work. Clea was—finally—taking the initiative. Reaching out to him.

In three days he was going to meet the man responsible for her terror of commitment. He couldn't very well pound him to a pulp in the august surroundings of La Marguerite. But he was fully prepared to hate his guts.

If he hadn't been stunned by lack of sleep and a nightmare so vivid he could still feel the weight of the chains, he'd have told Clea how brave she was. How much he appreciated the import of her phone call.

Wasn't it the first chink in her armor?

His thoughts marched on. She was willing to open her past to him, expose wounds that had gone frighteningly deep. He, Slade, couldn't add to that hurt. Couldn't dump her, to use her own words. It would be unconscionable. But—if they embarked on an affair—how could he avoid hurting her?

By marrying her? He couldn't do that if he didn't love her.

Start small, he thought. How about allowing her needs to supersede his for now? A whole new perspective for him: one that, at a level he scarcely understood, scared the wits out of him.

Sunlight gilded the Duomo. Through the glass he could hear the ceaseless roar of traffic. Quickly he rummaged for his palm pilot in his trouser pocket, and checked his appointments for the next few days. He had some rearranging to do if he was to be in Paris on Tuesday.

He'd do a lot more than cancel a meeting or two to understand why Clea was the way she was.

La Marguerite on Tuesday…it couldn't come quickly enough.

* * *

Paris was cold and wet, filled with bad-tempered Christmas shoppers and equally bad-tempered drivers. Rain slanted through the wide boulevards, pinging in the puddles, turning the roads into black mirrors and slowing the traffic to a crawl.

Gamely a tiered Christmas tree entirely made of lights glinted from the metal girders of the Eiffel Tower. The tree was topped with a brilliant star.

One moment Slade felt like that star, because Clea was opening her life to him. The next moment, though, he felt as cold as the sleety rain. She'd promised nothing other than an explanation. Explanations didn't necessarily entail change, or mean that she'd end the evening in his bed. And just who was the man she wanted him to meet?

Because Slade was impatient to see her, he was early at La Marguerite. Named for a flower, the restaurant surrounded an idyllic courtyard whose shrubs and trees sparkled with tiny white lights. Inside, cherrywood paneling and Fragonard-style murals were set off by gold chandeliers; thick carpeting muffled the sounds of conversation.

Slade was well acquainted with Gérard, the maître d', and was escorted to the table he was to share with Clea. Eight-thirty came and went; the restaurant started to fill up. Eight-thirty-five, eight-forty...had she changed her mind?

Then, with a tightening of his nerves, he saw her step into the entrance hall. The doorman took her long coat, and Gérard gave her a welcoming smile.

Not everyone who dared to be late at La Marguerite would be so generously welcomed.

As she was escorted to their table, Slade stood up. He was wearing his best Italian suit, a dark pinstripe, with the blue shirt and silk tie he'd worn at Belle's garden party.

But Clea wasn't looking at him; her gaze was skittering around the restaurant, checking out the occupants of every table, the look of strain on her face deepening. As Gérard pulled out her chair, Slade leaned forward and kissed her on both cheeks, making no attempt to hide how happy he was to see her.

Her dress was sea-green, long-sleeved, elaborately embroidered with silver thread; its neckline dipped low, a slender silver chain nestling between her breasts. Her hair was piled high on her head, stray tendrils caressing her cheeks.

He said huskily, "You take my breath away."

She blushed, taking her seat. "I look better than the last time you saw me."

She had yet to meet his eyes. He said matter-of-factly, "I gather the man we're to meet isn't here yet."

"No, not yet…I could have asked if he has a reservation for tonight, but Gérard's the epitome of discretion and probably wouldn't have told me…I'm sorry I'm so late, the plane was delayed and the traffic, as I'm sure you know, is horrendous."

She was speaking very fast, her fingers restlessly toying with the embossed menu. "It's called Christmas," Slade said dryly. "Why don't you decide what you want to eat, and then we'll talk?"

Quickly she chose truffle *feuilleté* followed by roast duck marinated in orange and coriander. Slade ordered a green salad served with chèvre, and *croustillant* of lamb; he picked a very dry red wine from the same château whose owner she had claimed to know. Clea was checking out the room again, noticing every arrival; her eyes were too bright, the color in her cheeks almost hectic.

Whoever the man was, he was foremost in Clea's thoughts. Slade sure wasn't.

Slade didn't care for this at all. He began describing a important contract he'd landed in Hamburg, her uneasiness transferring itself to him. What if tonight he found out something he really couldn't accept? What then?

Would he still take her to bed?

Their entrée plates were removed. Clea was drinking sparingly, and eating less. "If you don't eat your dinner," Slade said, "Gérard will be insulted."

She looked at him as though she wasn't sure who he was. He added brusquely, "Whoever this guy is, I sure hate the effect he has on you."

"Not half as much as I do," she muttered. "I'm sorry, Slade. I seem to be doing nothing but apologizing to you—how very tedious of me." She gave the waiter a bright, insincere smile as he put the roast duck in front of her. "That looks delicious," she said and stared down at it with something like loathing on her face.

The waiter put Slade's plate down with a flourish, topped up their wine glasses and disappeared. Clea picked up her fork, then suddenly dropped it with a clatter. A brown-haired man with a curvaceous blonde on his arm was approaching their table. Awkwardly Clea got to her feet, her serviette falling to the floor. In a voice Slade scarcely recognized, she faltered, "Papa?"

Papa, Slade thought, stunned. The mystery man was her father. His assumption that her parents were no longer living had been just that: an assumption. Clea had never actually told him they were dead.

He, too, stood up. But he might not have existed for all the attention Clea and her father were paying him. The man said in a voice as chilly as champagne, "Clea...well, what a surprise."

"I know you often eat here on Tuesdays," she said raggedly. "I thought I might see you."

"So this isn't a coincidence."

Trying to subdue a flood of rage that anyone, let alone her father, should speak to Clea with such brutal lack of feeling,

Slade said clearly, "*Bonsoir, M'sieur Chardin.* My name's Slade Carruthers."

"Raoul Chardin," the other man said with minimal politeness; he made no attempt to introduce the woman clinging to his arm, whose violet eyes were avariciously taking in every detail of Clea's appearance.

"Papa, can the four of us meet after dinner for a drink?" Clea asked. "It's been a long time since you and I have had the chance to talk."

"That wouldn't be convenient, no." He tugged at the blonde's fingers, which sparkled with an assortment of rings that could only be called garish. "Our table is ready, *chérie.* Come along."

The blonde said chirpily, "I'm Sylvie Tournier. I hadn't realized Raoul had a daughter...you must be younger than you look, Clea."

Clea gave her a blank look. "I'm twenty-six," she said. Then she turned back to her father. "How about tomorrow, Papa—I'm not leaving Paris until midafternoon. Could we meet for a coffee in the morning?"

She was openly begging. Clea, in Slade's experience of her, wasn't a woman to beg.

"I'm going back to the château in the morning," Raoul said curtly. "The vineyard doesn't run itself, you of all people should know that. Certainly you benefited from it financially for far too long."

"I haven't taken a penny of your money for years."

"Unlike your mother."

Clea flinched. "I'll call you the next time I come to Paris," she said. "Or I could visit you at the château."

"Perhaps. Sylvie, we're keeping Gérard waiting."

Sylvie gave Slade a look that was unquestionably a come-on. "I've heard about you," she said prettily. "I'm delighted to have made your acquaintance."

"Mam'selle Tournier, M'sieur Chardin," Slade said with cool formality and walked around the table to help Clea into her seat. Briefly he rested his hands on her shoulders, his fingers warm on her skin. Then he sat down himself.

He said crisply, "How could a man with ice-water in his veins have fathered a woman as passionate and full of life as you?"

She stabbed a piece of duck with her fork; tears were shimmering in her eyes. "I'm not passionate and full of life! I'm—to quote you—scared of my own shadow."

"That man's got as much feeling in him as a dead codfish. Has he ever given you the love a daughter should expect from her father?"

"No."

"But you keep hoping."

"Oh, yes—more fool me. Even when I'm begging him for five minutes of his precious time, I'm despising myself for asking." She took a sip of wine, her mouth twisted. "That's why I didn't ask him to meet us here tonight—he'd have refused. I had to leave it up to chance."

"Is your mother alive?" Clea nodded. "What's she like?"

Her lashes flickered. "You don't want to know."

"Yes, I do," Slade said mildly.

"Raoul's more than enough for one evening."

"He dyes his hair," Slade said.

She gave a choked laugh. "He has for years. That's one reason he doesn't want anything to do with me—Sylvie's younger than I am. The older he gets, the younger his mistresses."

"Sylvie will drop him in a flash when a bigger bank balance walks in the door."

Feeling minimally more cheerful, Clea said, "She'd drop him for you."

Slade shuddered. "I prefer redheads…did you live with your father until you were old enough to leave home?"

"No. He left first. When I was seven. The money he mentioned—that's how he discharged his parental duties. He stopped paying anything as soon as I turned sixteen."

"He doesn't love anyone but himself, Clea," Slade said gently.

Another tear gathered on her lashes. "I don't want to believe you. Which is really silly of me, I know."

"He withheld what you most needed from him…with the result that you're continually searching for it." Manfully Slade erased any anger from his voice. "Is he the reason you don't believe in commitment?"

Clea winced, the full import of her behavior washing over her. She'd meant this meeting with Raoul to be businesslike, cut and dried, with everything on the surface. Slade would meet her father, she'd describe some of Raoul's many mistresses and her own inability to commit would be tidily explained. Instead, her strategy had backfired: she'd humiliated herself in front of Slade by begging for her father's attention like a starving puppy. How could she have been so stupid?

"I can't tell you how many mistresses my father's had. I've lost count," she said in a brittle voice. "I have one of the wedding photos when he married my mother…they're gazing into each other's eyes in adoration. But by the time I was seven, they hated each other's guts. That's what marriage does, Slade. It changes people. Turns love to hatred."

"My mother and father still adore each other."

"Then they're the exception that proves the rule." She pushed an exquisitely glazed piece of meat around her plate. "I couldn't bear to have you speak to me the way my father does—that's why I'll never risk intimacy. Ever. And isn't that what commitment implies? Intimacy?"

It never had for him. Yet the scene Slade had just witnessed, which had roused in him a fury that went far beyond the casual, had unquestionably been intimate.

"Well," he said, leaning back in his chair, "at least I'm starting to understand where you're coming from."

"Five minutes in my father's company will do that."

"How about five seconds?" Slade smiled at her. An intimate smile, he realized, and wondered if he should be calling for help. "Try and eat something, Clea, you'll feel better if you do."

"When you look at me like that...I don't know how to handle it, Slade!"

"You don't have to handle anything. Eat up, we'll skip dessert and get the hell out of here—I don't even like being in the same room as your father."

"For once, we're in agreement," she said with a watery grin.

A few minutes later Slade signed the bill and slipped his credit card back in his wallet; he doubted that La Marguerite's admirable food had ever received so little attention. Getting to his feet, he pulled back Clea's chair. "Your father's hanging on to Sylvie's every word, not to mention her cleavage, and don't you dare look his way," he said in a conversational tone of voice. "In fact, why don't you gaze at me adoringly as though he's the last person on your mind? Sylvie will notice, even if he doesn't, and I'm sure she'll let him know."

Clea blinked. "That's deceitful."

He felt a bubble of laughter rise in his chest. "Try it—the adoring part—you might like it. You love me to distraction, darling Clea, and you can't wait to get me to your hotel room so you can strip the clothes from my back."

She was scowling at him. He added patiently, "Quit looking as though you want to strangle me. Rest your arm on my sleeve and kiss me—once will do. But be sure to keep upper-most in your mind a very wide bed with both of us in it. Stark naked."

"You're behaving extremely badly," Clea said, then reached up, her lips brushing his in a touch as delicate as gossamer. Briefly he cupped her face in his palms and kissed her back. "Mmm," he said, "roast duck."

Her sputter of laughter was unforced. "The last of the ro-mantics, that's you."

"I want you, I desire you, I need you," Slade said, naked truth edging his voice. "We'd better get out of here before I make love to you on the carpet."

"Gérard would have a heart attack," Clea said faintly.

"I imagine he would." Slade put his arm firmly around her waist and steered her toward the door. There he buttoned up her elegant long coat with its fur-edged hood, taking his time, his eyes lingering on her flushed features. Then he put on his raincoat and took his big umbrella, and they stepped out into the night.

Had he really said he needed her?

CHAPTER EIGHT

STANDING under the canopied entrance, Clea said quietly, "Thank you, Slade. For getting me out of there without—one more time—begging for a sideways glance from my father. I couldn't have done it alone."

It was a huge admission. "My pleasure. Want to walk for a while?"

"I would, yes." She tucked her arm in his as he put up the umbrella and they set off into the rain; to leave the vicinity of La Marguerite filled her with relief. "I could have told you about Raoul in Florence, I suppose—but having you meet him was probably more effective."

"You should congratulate me for not putting my famous left hook into practice—believe me, I was tempted. Why did he leave your mother, Clea?"

She might as well expose the whole sordid picture. "At the time, I had no idea. Another woman, I expect…when my mother told me he was leaving, I waylaid him at the door, pleaded with him to stay. He looked at me like I was dirt under his feet and asked why he would stay with a whining brat who hadn't even had the decency to be a boy."

"I should have decked him tonight. Gérard or no Gérard."

"I always feel about five years old when I'm anywhere near

him," she burst out. "It's so humiliating—even now I'd give my entire inheritance to have him say he loves me."

Rain pattered on the roof of Slade's umbrella; cars swished by, throwing up small fountains of spray. Clea talked on, filling in the portrait of the self-absorbed man who was her father. She almost never mentioned her mother, Slade noticed, filing this fact away for future reference.

They were approaching one of the metro's art nouveau entrances, with its fan of green-lit glass and intricately scrolled ironwork. Clea said impulsively, "Let's take the metro to Champs-Elysées—the Christmas decorations are always so pretty there. They'll look lovely in the rain."

She tugged at his sleeve, pulling him forward, smiling up at him. Slade's heart sank. He'd have done almost anything to keep that smile on her face. But ahead of him loomed the steep stairs with their iron railings, the dark cavity leading deeper and deeper under the ground. "I can't," he said.

"What do you mean? I've got tickets—come along."

She looked as excited as the little girl she'd once been. He said flatly, "I never take the metro. Or the New York subway or the London tube. I get—claustrophobic."

Her smile faded. She drew him to one side, keeping her grip on his sleeve, her eyes trained on his face. "Claustrophobic? Why?"

After the courage she'd shown tonight, she deserved the truth. He only hoped she wouldn't laugh her head off because he, a grown man, was scared to go down a few steps into the black tunnels of the Paris metro. "When I was eleven, I was kidnapped and held for ransom," he said rapidly. "Plucked off the street near my school, drugged, and kept in the basement in a dark cupboard for two weeks. Ever since then, I can't abide enclosed underground spaces."

"How were you rescued?" she whispered.

"Police and the FBI. I was one of the lucky ones."

Her eyes widened. "The bar!" she exclaimed in horror. "The Genoese. It's underground. Oh, Slade, I'm so sorry."

"It was probably good for me," he said. "Isn't that what all the pop psychology books advise—confront your fears?"

"Don't joke about something that's not remotely funny," Clea said fiercely, her words tumbling over each other. "If I'd known, I would never have suggested the Genoese…I can't believe you stayed there for three whole nights. If only I'd showed up on the first one—but I was so determined to test you, to prove myself right."

His smile was crooked. "You tested me, all right."

She didn't smile back. "You hung in," she said, touched to the core. "You didn't know me, you must have wondered if I'd keep my promise to show up. And yet you stayed there for three nights."

"Don't make me into some kind of knight errant," Slade said uncomfortably.

"I'm not. But I'm starting to realize how strong a man you are. How determined. I feel—" she sought for the right word "—humbled. That you should go through all that just because you want me."

"There's no *just* about it."

Ignoring him, she said slowly, "Your courage…and your integrity. I haven't wanted to see you as you really are, because then I can't dismiss you as easily." Unconsciously her fingers tightened on his sleeve. "I don't understand why you want me so much—and no, I'm not fishing for compliments."

"I don't understand, either," he said roughly. "All I know is that you haunt me day and night, I can't sleep because you're not beside me, and I don't even want to look at another woman."

"Well," she said shakily, "that's plenty."

"But then there's the C word. Commitment."

"By now I thought you'd understand why that word drives me crazy! My father changes women as easily as he changes his tie. The men I go around with—their affairs are turned on and off like the kitchen tap, because there's always another beautiful woman around the corner."

Hit by a sudden insight, Slade said, "You don't trust me to abide by the terms I'm setting up. To be faithful to you."

"Why would I?" she flashed, knowing he'd unearthed one more layer to her resistance. "Nothing in my background or my present life leads me to believe men are trustworthy."

"If I can last three nights at the Genoese, I can handle commitment to you for as long as we're an item, Clea."

"An item," she said bitterly, "an affair—I even hate the language."

"An exploration," he heard himself say. "A voyage of discovery. Maybe we'll be lousy in bed together. Maybe you take all the covers."

"Or snore," she said with a sudden grin. "I bet you drop used towels all over the bathroom floor."

"And expect you to pick them up." His smile faded. "Clea, I desire you with every fiber of my being. As I believe you desire me. We'd be fools to pass that up because we're afraid of what might happen."

"You'll get what you want and then you'll leave," she said in a stony voice.

"I won't," he said, hearing the two little words echo in his head. "But I can't prove that until after we've made love."

"By which time it's too late."

Her shoulders were drooping, her face drained of its usual vivacity. Could he hope to defeat, even temporarily, the damage Raoul and his like had inflicted on her? "You're tired," Slade said.

She was; her father always had that effect on her. "I'd like to go back to my hotel."

"There's a taxi stand just down the street."

When they were seated, Clea quickly gave the name of her hotel. Then she leaned back, closing her eyes. Her profile flashed in and out against the streetlights, her hair seeming to weigh down her slender neck. Slade put his arm around her. Despite all the power and money at his command, and no matter how much he wanted to, he couldn't make Raoul Chardin give her what she craved.

Twenty minutes later they drew up outside an eighteenth century mansion south of the Seine, its tall black-painted doors flanked by boxwood in terra-cotta pots. "Clea," Slade said, squeezing her shoulder, "we're here."

She roused herself, rubbing her eyes. "Will you come in?" she asked.

He had no idea what she was thinking. "Sure," he said, and paid the driver.

She led him through a long tree-lined passageway into an open courtyard. "I love this hotel," she remarked, talking fast. "It's like the one in Copenhagen, small enough to be intimate. The gardens in summer are exquisite, and from here I can easily walk along the river, then across the bridge to Jardins des Tuileries."

Once again she was nervous, he thought, as they entered the charming lobby with its antique furnishings and air of quiet comfort. Without looking to see if he was following, Clea headed straight for the elevators, and within moments they were walking along the corridor to her suite. She ushered him inside, and made quite a business of hanging up their coats and spreading the umbrella wide so it would dry. She looked as brittle as a Dresden figurine, Slade thought in a rush of protectiveness. "I'm going to ask the obvious—why did you bring me up here?"

"I don't know," she said jerkily, striving to be as honest with him as she knew how. "Maybe I thought I could finally do it. Make the leap. Trust you enough to go to bed with you."

Heaven knew he wanted that. But just as strongly he was convinced tonight wasn't the night. "You're exhausted, your father upset you—"

"Do I look that bad?"

"You look like you'd shatter into a thousand pieces if I said *boo*."

She kicked off her shoes, walked up to him with none of her usual grace and rested her forehead on his chest. "Hold on to me," she said in a muffled whisper.

He put his arms around her, drawing her close to his body, his cheek resting on her sweetly scented hair. Only gradually did he realize she was crying, slow tears soaking through his shirtfront. Knowing exactly what he was going to do, he picked her up and carried her through the sitting room with its rose-pink Aubusson carpet into the bedroom. The bed was a four-poster covered in ruffled white eyelet. Putting her down, he reached for the zipper on the back of her dress. "Where's your nightgown?" he said matter-of-factly.

"Under the pillow. Slade—"

"Hush," he said. "This is getting to be a habit, undressing you and then walking out the door. Talk about a test."

"You're not staying?"

Was he imagining that hint of relief in her voice? "No."

She reached for a tissue and blew her nose. "Yankee cussedness versus Parisian lust."

He passed her the silk gown, which was the color of café au lait, turning his back as she stood up to remove her dress and slip on the nightgown. "How about common sense coupled with admiration for your courage?" he said. "I like that version better."

"Courage? When I'm still afraid?"

"Yes. Courage."

"You mean you still want me?" she said in a low voice. "Now that you've met my father?"

He turned around; she was sitting on the bed. "Clea, I want you so badly I can taste it. Yeah, the Genoese was a test. But—trust me—for me to walk out of here tonight is almost more than I can bear."

Shivering, she muttered, "I wish you wouldn't say things like that."

"I say them because they're true." His smile was rueful. "They take me by surprise, too."

She blurted, "Once we go to bed, this crazy attraction between us will fizzle out."

"Do you honestly believe that?" Not waiting for a reply, Slade said forcefully, "When we make love, I'll enter every cell of your body. And you'll encompass every cell of mine. That's how it'll be—I know it, and, deep down, so do you."

Her eyes were downcast; her gown was clinging to her breasts, her skin pale ivory. And what a lot of skin, Slade thought, taking in the vulnerable slope of shoulder, the graceful curve of arm, her high-arched bare feet. To walk away from her was going to take more strength than he possessed.

He sat down beside her, took her face in his hands and kissed her mouth with slow sensuality, savoring her, letting all his pleasure show as he slid his fingers down her throat to her bare shoulders. Her surrender was instant, yet oddly gentle, like spring rain. His heart overflowing with an emotion new to him, one he wasn't sure he could name, Slade nibbled at her lips. "Fizzle out, did you say? Not a chance…"

Clea put her palms flat to his chest, pushing him away. "Every time you kiss me, I change," she cried. "I go up and down like the stock market. The way I behave, the things I say, the feelings I have when I'm with you—I never know what I'm going to do next."

"Life demands change of us," he said roughly. "And change is difficult."

"My father's never changed," she whispered.

"That's right. And likely never will. Is that what you want for *your* life?"

"You're so relentless," she said, the heat from his skin burning into her fingers. "Is that how you got to the top?"

He moved his shoulders restlessly, once again allowing the truth to spill out. "I'm not just fighting for me here—I'm fighting for you, too. If you turn your back on me, we both lose." He smoothed her forehead with his lips. "Do something for me—meet me at Kennedy Airport in New York City right after the New Year. I'll take you for the most fabulous lunch you've ever eaten, and that includes every Michelin-starred restaurant in France."

Her head reared back. "Your parents live in New York City."

"They do."

"Just because you've met my father doesn't mean I want to meet them."

"So far, you and I have gotten together in Monte Carlo, Copenhagen, Florence and Paris. Three of those cities were your choice. Now it's my turn."

"You make it sound so reasonable."

"That's me—reasonable."

She made a rude sound. "I'm out of my mind. Yes, I'll meet you in Manhattan."

Trying to mask a relief that scared him with its force, Slade said, "Once you've booked, let me know your flight time. I've got meetings after the fourth of January that I can't put off, but until then I'm free. And wear something warm—Trinidad to New York in winter is a shocker."

"A dress-up lunch?" she asked.

"Just as long as you turn up, I don't give a damn what you wear." He leaned forward and kissed her again. "Good night, Clea."

The question was out before she could censor it. "You're really going to leave?"

"Have you changed your mind about commitment?"

"Commitment's the very opposite of freedom."

Almost sure she sounded less convinced by that magical word *freedom*, Slade said tautly, "I stayed the course at the bar. I've rearranged my schedules and jetted all over Europe for you. I'm doing my level best right now not to use sex as a weapon. What the hell else do you want from me?"

"I don't know!"

"When you figure it out, we'll go to bed," he said in a hard voice. Getting up, he jammed his hands in his pockets. "Until then, I'm going to keep on walking away from you even though it half-kills me every time."

"Me, too."

The quiver in her voice went right through him. "God, Clea, the last thing I want to do is fight with you after the night you've had. Get into bed, pull the covers up to your chin so I can't see all that enticing flesh, and go to sleep."

In a flash of bare thighs she slipped under the puffy white duvet. "I'll see you in New York," she said.

"In the meantime, happy Christmas. Enjoy Trinidad."

Leaning over, he switched out the bedside lamp. The darkness giving her courage, Clea announced, "Until I met you, I was always the one calling the shots."

He laughed. "You know what? The same's true of me."

"We can't both call the shots."

"If we want the same thing, we can…good night, captivating Clea."

"*Bonsoir,* sexy Slade."

His eyes adjusting to the gloom, he strode toward the door of the suite. His whole body ached with frustration. He'd walk all the way to his hotel, which was across the Seine in the Opéra Quarter.

Perhaps it would take his mind off sex. Off the beautiful redhead alone in her hotel room, where he'd left her.

The woman who was changing his life.

It was the third day of the new year. The plane from Miami was half an hour late, and there were delays in customs. Gradually a slow trickle of travelers started coming through the frosted glass doors, their tans ranging from copper to scorched pink.

Then Clea walked into the arrivals area. She was wearing turquoise wool pants with a matching collarless long coat; an off-white turtleneck sweater hugged her throat. Slade waved his present at her to get her attention, and watched her smile, a dazzling smile that made his heart thud in his chest.

As she eased through the crowds toward him, he saw that she was wearing the earrings he'd given her, small gold birds with their wings outspread. Then she was standing in front of him. "Is that for me?" she asked.

He was carrying a six-foot-tall stuffed giraffe with a big red-and-green bow tied around its neck. "Merry late Christmas," he said, wrapped his arms around her and the giraffe, and kissed her with a pent-up passion that spoke volumes.

When she emerged, she looked thoroughly flustered. "You still want me," she said.

"That's one of the things I like about you—your grasp of the essentials." His smile felt as wide as the giraffe's neck was long. He held it out to her. "His name is George."

Her laugh was a joyful ripple. "What am I supposed to do with him?"

"Put him in your apartment," Slade said promptly, "and whenever you look at him, think of me."

"My apartment is furnished in minimalist style."

"I figured it was. He'll brighten the place up."

"One more step in your campaign?"

"Campaign? What campaign?"

She was gazing into the giraffe's face. "I wish I had eyelashes like his."

"Your eyelashes—along with the rest of you—are perfect, Clea," Slade said huskily, his eyes drinking in every detail of her features.

Clea gave a tiny shiver. How could she resist him, so ardent, so intense? Tucking the giraffe under her arm, she pulled Slade's head down and kissed him with an explicitness that spoke volumes. He said unsteadily, "I guess that means you still want me."

She compressed her lips. "I guess it does. A bit. Sometimes."

"Live dangerously—say yes."

"All right, yes. Yes, I do want you. In Trinidad I even found myself wishing you were with me. You'd have loved the beach, Slade, it was in a sheltered cove and every morning the frigate birds swam there, and once I saw a green turtle..."

While they waited for her luggage, she talked animatedly, Slade watching the play of expression on her face with its delicate tan. Would she ever capitulate and open her arms to him? And if so, would he ever have enough of her?

Outside, the ground was bare and the wind sharp. Clea hugged the giraffe to her, shivering for a different reason. "We should have met in the Bahamas."

His car was in the parking lot, a sleek Mercedes coupe.

Sinking into the leather seat, she said, "Mmm…nice. Where are we going for lunch?"

"Uptown," he said evasively. "Tell me about your friends in Trinidad."

The traffic was heavy, but by one o'clock he was driving along Madison Avenue. Turning onto a side street, he parked by the curb. "We're here," he said.

"I don't see any restaurants," Clea said, her brow furrowed with suspicion.

"We're having lunch with my parents. Smoked salmon fish cakes with rhubarb chutney."

"Dirty trick, Slade."

"All part of the campaign, Clea. I'm showing you the opposite side of the coin from your parents' marriage."

Her temper climbed another notch. "I wondered if you'd want me to meet your parents while I was here. But I never thought you'd take me there for lunch without checking with me first."

"I didn't check because I knew you'd say no."

"I can still say no."

"But you won't. Admit it, you're curious to meet them. To see if they're real, this saintly couple who are still in love after nearly forty years."

"See the sights of New York—the Empire State Building, the Faithful Couple," she said crazily.

"You'll like them—I swear you will."

"You take far too much for granted!"

"Not you, Clea," he said hoarsely. "Never you." And bit his tongue in exasperation. Why did he persist in mouthing feelings he hadn't previously known?

She let out her breath in a small sigh. "Can I take the giraffe in with me?"

"You want to embarrass me in front of my parents?"

"It would give me considerable satisfaction to do so."

They got out, Clea clutching the giraffe to her chest as Slade locked the car. The elevator carried them smoothly to the top floor. Slade said nothing the whole way up. When they arrived, Clea planted her feet in the wide hallway. "You're nervous," she said in sudden discovery.

"Yeah."

"I talk too much when I'm nervous, and you clam up."

"That's because I'm from New England."

"Let's hope your parents aren't nervous, too. Or it'll be a very quiet lunch." Frowning, she added, "Just what have you told them about me?"

"That I met you at Belle's. That they'll like you...that's about it."

Her frown deepened. "Why do I get the impression you're omitting something?"

"You're too clever by half."

"Come clean."

"You're the first woman I've ever brought here," he admitted. "For lunch, dinner or breakfast. I know that and so, of course, do they."

Dismayed, Clea said, "They probably think we're in love. Planning to get married."

"Then they'd be wrong on both counts, wouldn't they?"

"You're darn right." She tossed her head, hiding a sudden and unexpected shaft of pain that Slade, despite wanting her so badly, wasn't even remotely in love with her.

Not that she wanted him to be in love with her.

He said abruptly, "Why are you wearing the earrings I gave you?"

"So you won't forget I need my freedom."

Inwardly he winced; hadn't he hoped she'd been wearing them for sentimental reasons? "You tell it like it is, don't you?" he said, unable to erase the edge in his voice. "Shall I ring the bell?"

"Do," she said sweetly. "The housekeeper we had when I was six did her best to instill good manners into me—I promise I'll behave."

The housekeeper, he thought. Not her father or her mother. Reaching around her, Slade rang the doorbell.

CHAPTER NINE

SLADE'S father swung the door open. "Slade—and you must be Clea. Do come in."

David Carruthers was nearly as tall as his son, his build athletic, his hair a distinguished gray. His blue eyes were full of life. He introduced himself to Clea, giving her the full benefit of his smile.

Clea said the first thing that came to mind. "You look astonishingly like your son."

David laughed. "Twenty-five years older—a minor detail. Uh...that's a fine giraffe."

"His name is George," Clea said limpidly, setting the giraffe down in the corner. "My Christmas gift from Slade."

"Anyone can buy sweaters and jewelry," Slade said with a lazy grin. "Hello, Mum."

"Slade, darling," Bethanne said, kissing him on the cheek with unaffected love, her patrician features flushed with pleasure. Then she turned to Clea. "Welcome, Clea," she said, wiping her hands on her ruffled apron before shaking hands with Clea. "I'm so glad you could join us today."

Although her words were conventional, the warmth behind them was genuine, Clea sensed that immediately. David said easily, "Here, let me take your coat...Slade said you've just flown in from Trinidad."

The talk gathered momentum as they walked into the spacious living room, with its panoramic view of the bare-limbed trees of Central Park. Bethanne's eye for color was everywhere evident, from the glowing hues of the Persian rug to the rich red cushions on the navy-blue chesterfield. Impressionistic art adorned the walls; a small jungle of tropical plants was grouped near the windows.

David offered Clea a drink; Bethanne brought out broiled shrimp and a dip; and Slade sat down with his back to the light, where he could watch Clea. This room was as familiar to him as the office downtown where he spent so much of his time; to have Clea sitting in it was disconcerting.

Her fiery red hair clashed with the cushions.

"An incredible martini," she said to David. "And, Bethanne, the shrimp are luscious."

"David can also make plants flourish indoors and out; and steer a kayak down a raging torrent, emerging right way up at the other end," Bethanne teased. "Rivers with big waves on them make me run for cover—but I love to garden. You've seen Belle Hayward's garden, Clea…it's lovely, isn't it? She's an old friend of ours."

Clea smiled her assent, and segued to some of the famous gardens she'd visited in Europe. The conversation moved from topic to topic, Clea neatly fielding any questions that approached her private life.

As they got up to move into the dining room, Slade said curiously, "The painting in the corner—it's new, isn't it?"

"David gave it to me for our anniversary," Bethanne said, giving her husband an unselfconscious hug. "I adore it. Just look how the sun falls on the water…"

"Thirty-nine years," David said, smiling into his wife's blue eyes. "And each one better than the last."

Clea's mouth tightened, her eyes suddenly liquid with pain.

Her lashes dropped; absently, she brushed her fingertips over the glossy leaves of a fig tree. Then, as if she felt Slade's gaze on her, she looked right at him. The pain had vanished from her eyes as if it had never been. He said hastily, "Good choice, Dad. Did I tell you I'm bidding on a small Ghiberti bronze? Early fifteenth century."

"For the Florence house?" Bethanne asked. "Have you been there, Clea?"

Heat rose in Clea's cheeks. "Oh—er, yes, I have."

"Just once," Slade said.

"You must get him to cook for you there," Bethanne went on, starting to ladle out a thick leek soup. "His kitchen is a dream."

"He made soup for me," Clea said. And looked after me, she thought, the memory bittersweet.

"I taught Slade the difference between basil and oregano at a very early age," Bethanne remarked. "I was determined not to bring up a son who thinks the kitchen is solely for women."

"Not a hope, Mum," Slade said.

He passed freshly baked cheese sticks and talked at some length about his latest project near Hamburg; Bethanne brought in smoked salmon fish cakes with rhubarb chutney. Clea said, "You're famous for these, so Slade told me. In Trinidad we ate fish cakes made from shark…"

She began describing some of the meals they'd had in the beach house over Christmas. It was, Slade thought, a rather unsubtle message that she had many friends, and had chosen not to spend Christmas with David and Bethanne's son. He replenished everyone's wine, and changed the subject to the hurricanes that had lashed Florida last September.

When they were finished with the fish cakes, which had indeed been delicious, Bethanne and David got up to clear the table for dessert. As they carried plates into the kitchen, Clea also got up, taking the dish of chutney and the basket of cheese sticks from the table. Slade followed with the side plates. In the kitchen, Bethanne was rinsing the plates under the tap, David standing very close to her, his arm around her waist, his lips nuzzling her ear.

Clea stopped dead in her tracks. Slade cleared his throat. "Okay, you two, break it up."

Bethanne gave a little start. "Oh, I didn't mean for you to help," she said, flustered. "David, stop!"

Her husband patted her on the bottom. "Whatever you say, sweetheart. Should I whip the cream?"

"That would be a good idea," Bethanne said firmly, and took the plates from Slade. "The chutney goes back in that jar, Clea, and the cheese sticks in the bag on the counter."

Dessert was a compote of fruit laced with Grand Marnier and slathered with cream. David tucked in, winking at his son. "Back to skim milk tomorrow," he said.

Clea launched determinedly into a discussion of the latest fads in diets. Coffee was produced and drunk. Bethanne took Clea on a tour of the penthouse; David discussed plans for repairs to the Maine house. And then, finally, it was time to leave.

Clea thanked his parents with a pleasure Slade would have sworn was unfeigned. "I hope we see you again soon," Bethanne said, kissing Clea lightly on both cheeks.

"That would be delightful," David added. "Talk to you in a couple of days, Slade, when I've got the estimate for the roof."

"Great, Dad...thanks, Mum."

"Love you," Bethanne said, as she always did when they parted, whether for ten minutes or two months.

Clea picked up George the giraffe, and she and Slade went downstairs in the elevator. She tossed the giraffe in the back of the car before getting in the passenger seat. As Slade slammed his door, she said with icy politeness, "Shall we fight now or later?"

Her eyes were the blue of a glacier. "Now," Slade said, and went on the attack. "My parents are real people, Clea. They haven't always had it easy. Their families never got along…the kidnapping was a terrible time for them…they always wanted more children but Mum had a series of miscarriages instead. And, I'm sure, they've had the usual difficulties of any long-term marriage. But they love each other deeply, and that's carried them through—it's called commitment."

"The perfect antidote for my father."

"Okay, so bringing you here for lunch wasn't overly subtle of me. But I'm not going to hide my parents just because they happen to be in love."

"They can't keep their hands off each other," she cried. "They were necking—at their age—in the kitchen."

"They do it all the time. I look the other way…I don't want to know about my parents' sex life, thank you very much. But what's their age got to do with it? Don't you think you could be the same?"

"No, I don't!"

"I can only think of one way to prove you wrong," he said incautiously.

"And what's that?"

"For you and me to live together for thirty-nine years and then have this argument again."

His words hung in the air. What had possessed him to say them? He'd never wanted to live with anyone, for one year or thirty-nine. And now he was suggesting living with Clea? Obstinate and argumentative Clea?

Desirable, fiery, beautiful Clea…

She glared at him. "Stop treating me like a big joke!"

"That's not my intention. All I did today was introduce you to two people who've loved each other through thick and thin. To show you it can be done with grace and courage, and that the end result is happiness."

As had so often happened, Slade had sliced the ground from under her feet. "Okay, so I've never met anyone like them before. And I get your point—people can stay married and be happy. Or at least, your parents have been able to do so." And how it had hurt, she thought, to see such deep, unaffected and enduring love.

With fierce intensity she went on, "I don't know how to do what they've done. I never learned. I had no models. So marriage is the last thing I'd ever embark on." She took a short, sharp breath. "I hardly dare ask what's the next step in your campaign."

"Get you into bed," he said promptly. "Without that stupid giraffe watching our every move."

"Then we'll live together for thirty-nine years? Very funny," she said tightly. "The next step in the campaign is mine—do you have plans for tomorrow?"

"Nope. I leave for Oslo the day after."

She snapped open her purse, took out a small pad and pen and her cell phone, and punched in some numbers. Then she spoke in very rapid Italian, waited a couple of minutes for a reply and jotted down some numbers on the pad. *"Grazie... arrivederci."*

She passed the pad to Slade. "That was my travel agent. You and I are flying to Kentucky tomorrow morning. Lexington."

"To meet your mother," he said intuitively.

"Precisely. You might as well know the whole sorry story—and no, I'm not going to talk about her. You'll meet her soon enough."

"Let's go for a walk," Slade said abruptly. "Too much to eat and too much emotion in the last couple of hours."

"I have an appointment at a bank downtown."

"Then we'll meet after that."

She said, her heart racing in her breast, "I can't. I'm having dinner with a friend."

His gut clenched. "Male or female?"

"He looks after a portion of my portfolio. I've known him for years."

So angry he could scarcely talk, Slade grated, "Do I mean anything at all to you, Clea? Or am I as disposable as all your other men?"

"I don't know what you mean to me, that's the whole problem." It was absurd of her to feel guilty. So why did she? "This was a good opportunity to see Tom, that's all," she said. "I'll take a cab to my appointment."

"You do that. Have fun explaining the giraffe at the bank."

"Having lots of money means you don't have to explain," she retorted, her cheeks bright pink.

Moments later she was marching away from him toward Madison Avenue to hail a cab, the giraffe's long legs sticking out behind her, the smaller of her two suitcases in her other hand. Slade banged his fist on the steering wheel. Right now she was calling the shots, and how he hated it.

Tomorrow he was going to meet her mother.

The Darthley Stud Farm was nestled in Kentucky bluegrass country, near Lexington. Classic, Slade thought, as he and Clea drove along a winding paved road between white-painted rail fences, the branches of massive oak and beech trees black against a gray sky. Mares and foals were clustered around loose piles of hay near an immaculately maintained barn. Every one of the horses looked healthy and exceedingly well-bred.

He'd been disinclined to make small talk ever since he'd met Clea at the airport. He flat-out refused to inquire if she'd enjoyed her dinner; nor was he going to ask if the man who managed her portfolio was thirty-five or sixty-five.

Let her do the talking.

But Clea, the closer they got to the stud farm, became equally quiet. As they drew up outside a magnificent brick mansion wreathed in wisteria, she finally broke the silence. "I called my mother this morning. She's expecting us. The name she goes by is Lucie DesRoches, even though she was born Amy Payton in Pittsburgh, Pennsylvania. Byron Darthley, who owns all this, is her eighth husband."

Then she got out of the car. This morning she was wearing a severely cut pair of dark gray wool trousers with a moss-green cashmere blazer and a white silk blouse; small gold hoops hung at her lobes. Her hair was ruthlessly tugged into a knot on the back of her head, although Slade was heartened to see several stray strands curling on her nape.

Eighth husband, he thought. No thirty-ninth wedding anniversaries for Lucie DesRoches.

Clea pushed hard on the doorbell. It was opened by the butler, his face as sour as last month's milk; he led them into an overdecorated and completely soulless living room and left them there. She paced up and down, picking up an ornament, putting it down, checking her hair in the mirror, twitching at the hem of her blazer, and wishing she were anywhere else but here.

"Clea...what a nice surprise."

The first thing Slade noticed was that Lucie DesRoches was an outstandingly beautiful woman; the second, that it was taking considerable effort to maintain that beauty. Her russet hair was expensively dyed, her makeup a work of art and her clothes, rather too fussy for a morning in the country, reeked of money.

"Hello, Mother," Clea said, and took a step toward Lucie,

her hands tentatively outstretched. Casually Lucie retreated behind a spindly antique table; Clea dropped her hands to her sides, schooling her face to a protective mask.

So that's the story, Slade thought, unsurprised, and said calmly, "How do you do, Mrs. DesRoches...I'm Slade Carruthers, a friend of Clea's."

Lucie transferred her emerald-green eyes to Slade. Contacts, he thought unkindly, and smiled down at her.

"Why, Clea, honey," she drawled, "you got yourself a real prize here. How do you do, Mr. Carruthers—or may I call you Slade? And please call me Lucie, we don't stand much on ceremony in these parts."

She put her palm in his, squeezing his hand just a touch too meaningfully. "I'm pleased to meet you, Lucie," he said. "You have a lovely place here."

Discontent dragged at the corners of her mouth. "Nice of you to say so. I wanted Byron to refurbish the entire downstairs, but he insisted on buying another stallion instead. Four million dollars for one horse when the country club down the road has better drapes than I do."

"Where is Byron?" Clea asked.

"In the barn. Where else would you find him?"

"The horses are in great shape," Slade interjected.

"So's the new stablehand," Lucie said waspishly. "A girl. In her early twenties."

"Mother..."

"Don't you *Mother* me, Clea! Byron's always had wandering eyes, and now the rest of him's in on the act. What he doesn't understand is that I'm keeping tabs on him and passing it all on to my lawyer."

"Not another lawyer," Clea said, her heart sinking. "You were madly in love with Byron a couple of years ago."

Lucie's eyes filled with decorative tears. "It's a terrible

thing when a man turns his back on his vows, Slade—wouldn't you agree?"

"Yes," he said, "it is."

"Have you ever been married?" He shook his head. "You planning on marrying my Clea?" Her voice quavered. "I had her when I was almost a child."

He said evasively, "I see where she gets her beauty."

"Why, thank you," Lucie simpered. "Clea, why don't you get Byron? I told him we'd have sherry in the drawing room. But I guess he's got other things on his mind, like that little bitch in the stables—he doesn't pay much attention to me anymore."

"Certainly, Mother," Clea said and fled the room as though sixteen stallions were about to trample her.

Lucie poured a glass of sherry from a Baccarat decanter and passed it to Slade. Then she put her hand on his sleeve, directing the full force of her emerald eyes at him. Deliberately she moved closer, until her breast brushed his arm. He fought the impulse to run out of the room after Clea, and stepped back.

Lucie's fingers tightened until he could feel the bands of her rings digging into his flesh. "Clea's way too young for you, honey," she breathed. "You look like a man who'd appreciate a mature woman. Someone ripe and understanding…"

"It's Clea I want," Slade said loudly. "Unfortunately commitment is a dirty word to her."

Venom thinned Lucie's mouth. "The difference between Clea and me is that she doesn't have the decency to marry her men. She uses them and tosses them aside like they're no more than an outfit she's bought."

From the corner of his eye Slade saw a tiny movement near the door. Clea was standing there, and must have heard every word. He said curtly, "I don't believe that to be true of her."

"Then for all your handsome face, you're a fool," Lucie snapped. "Clea, sugar, is Byron coming?"

Clea stepped inside, wishing she could erase from her mind the sight of the buxom brunette locked in her stepfather's embrace against the paddock fence. "He says he can't spare the time."

"Did you meet darling little Kimberley?"

"Why don't we have a drink?" Clea said. "We don't need Byron."

"So you did meet her." Lucie snapped the stopper from the decanter again and sloshed amber sherry into two more of the long-stemmed glasses; for a moment, Slade was convinced that the emotion that had flickered across Lucie's perfect features was nothing short of terror. He passed Clea a glass, took a healthy gulp of an excellent Spanish dry sherry, and determinedly steered the conversation into safer channels. Half an hour later, he and Clea took their leave.

Quickly Clea brushed her lips to Lucie's cheek. "Take care of yourself, Mother."

"Don't talk to me as if I was in my dotage," Lucie snapped. Switching on a smile, she added, "A pleasure to have met you, Slade. You remember what I said."

"Goodbye, Lucie," he said, and hoped the note of finality in his voice was as obvious to her and Clea as it was to him.

The big door swung shut behind them. Clea marched to their car and Slade slid behind the wheel. As they drove past the first bend in the road, Clea said bitterly, "She put the move on you, didn't she? My own mother!"

"Yeah," he said. "But you must have heard what I said."

"I'm so ashamed of her," Clea muttered. "She cheapens everything."

"She didn't cheapen either me or you, Clea. No one can do that to us."

"She doesn't know the meaning of love. Or vow. Or fidelity. Would you like me to tell you what it was like growing up with my mother and her succession of men?"

"Go ahead," Slade said evenly.

"The man I call my father—because who knows if he really is?—was number two. I don't remember number one, she met him at a debutante ball and the marriage lasted exactly six months. I was an accident, by the way, so she told me as soon as I was old enough to understand. She never wanted me. After all, I'd ruined her figure."

Slade pulled over to the side of the road and turned off the ignition. "Who was number three and how long did he last?"

"A Spanish bullfighter. A year and a half, when it became as obvious to Lucie as to everyone else that he loved the Plaza de Toros a lot more than he loved my mother. Number four was an Austrian businessman, who tried to take the wildness out of me by a combination of discipline and terror tactics."

"For God's sake, Clea…"

"I hated him. But then she married Pete. He was a sailor, he owned a racing yacht that was the most beautiful boat I've ever seen. We lived in a cedar house by the ocean in British Columbia, and I had the run of the woods and the shore, and for two whole years I was happy…" Her face clouded. "Mum had already started divorce proceedings—living in the woods wasn't her scene—when he drowned in a freak accident."

Slade sat very still. "How old were you?"

"Thirteen. I was shipped off to boarding school in Switzerland and Mother took up with an Italian art collector. I graduated at seventeen, inherited enough of my grandfather's trust at eighteen to set up my own apartment in Milan, and the rest is history…oh, yes, there was a Swiss banker after the art collector and before Byron—have I missed anyone?"

"I can understand why you're bitter, Clea—it's a wonder to me you didn't plunge knee-deep into booze and drugs."

"I tried getting really drunk just once when I was young. But it made me so sick I decided it wasn't for me. And I've never done drugs. I like being in control too much, I guess."

"For once, I'm all for you being in control." He took her hands in his, gently rubbing her slender, ringless fingers. "Your mother's running scared, Clea—she knows she's getting older, that she can't keep up this kind of lifestyle. Yet she's got nothing to replace it with."

"Byron's a sleaze, I thought that the first time I met him. But he has tons of money."

Slade asked something that subconsciously had been bothering him for a while. "Why did your grandfather leave his money to you, and not to your mother?"

"He was a straitlaced old tyrant who didn't condone divorce. My mother inherited my grandmother's fortune instead—peanut butter and mustard pickles. One more reason Mother changed her name from Payton to DesRoches."

"One more reason she resents you?" Clea nodded. "You said your father vanished from the scene when you were seven."

"Mother sent me to stay with him the first summer after the divorce, so she'd have a clear field—or should I say arena?—for the bullfighter. Raoul was furious. He left me in the care of his horrendous old housekeeper, who threatened me with dungeons and rats. I ran away and refused to stay with him ever again."

Despite her best intentions, she was trembling. But when Slade put his arm around her shoulder, she pulled away. "Let's go back to the airport," she said in a dull voice. "I hate being within ten miles of my mother."

To remove her from the vicinity of the Darthley Stud Farm seemed an eminently sensible idea to Slade, and she'd given him plenty to think about. Besides, it would give her time to collect herself.

She'd had a lot of practice doing that, he thought, his heart aching for the little red-haired girl who'd been dragged from country to country and stepfather to stepfather; only once had she been given anything other than indifference and outright hostility.

No wonder she was wary of commitment; finally he understood the source and depth of her antipathy.

He drove on through the rolling countryside. They'd spend the night in his apartment in Manhattan, he decided. He'd rustle up something for supper, and do his level best to banish the stricken look from Clea's eyes.

However, just before they reached the airport, his cell phone rang. He flipped it open. "Carruthers," he said. Then his voice sharpened. "Backing out? *Why?*"

Clea glanced over at him. His jaw was a hard line, his fingers clenched around the phone. The ruthless businessman, she thought with an inward shiver; plainly she herself had vanished from his mind.

The conversation lasted a couple more minutes, then Slade said, "You've organized a jet for Lexington? I'll leave right away. Thanks, Bill."

He folded the cell phone and thrust it in his pocket. "That was my assistant. I'll have to fly straight to Oslo. There's been a major screwup and four months' work could go down the drain." He moved his shoulders restlessly. "I'm sorry, Clea—more sorry than I can say—to leave you now, so soon after seeing your mother."

The feeling uppermost in Clea's body was relief. She could be alone, she thought. She could regroup, figure out what she was going to do about the man sitting so close to her in the car. The man who knew more about her than anyone else in the world. She said evenly, "It's okay, I understand how important your work is to you."

His work was important to him. All-important. So why did he feel torn in two at the prospect of leaving her? "Where will you go?" he demanded.

"Oh, back to Europe, I expect," she said vaguely. "Skiing, maybe. The powder's great in the Alps at this time of year."

"Europe and the Alps cover a lot of territory," Slade rapped. "Can you be a bit more specific?"

"St. Moritz, or possibly Chamonix."

He pulled up in the rental area and turned off the ignition. "Let Bill know what you decide. He keeps track of the various phone numbers where I can be reached."

As she made a noncommittal noise, he added impatiently, "Do it, Clea. We're past the stage of playing cat and mouse, for God's sake."

"All right, I will," she said, over an immense lethargy. Her mother's coldness, Byron's infidelity...which was worse? David and Bethanne, with their happy marriage, seemed a million miles away. "Where do you go to find your jet?"

"It should be out on the tarmac. I'll have to go through customs."

Slade got out of the car. For the first time in his life, he found himself resenting the demands of his own corporation. He didn't want to fly to Oslo. He wanted to be with Clea. It was that simple, and that complicated. "Come in with me, while I find out what the score is," he said.

Ten minutes later, he was ready to go through customs. Standing by the door, Slade took Clea in his arms, rubbing her taut shoulders; her mask, the mask he hated, was very much in place. But he had to go to Oslo. He had to. He said, sounding brusque and efficient rather than concerned, "Look after yourself, won't you? I'll be in touch in a couple of days."

Her smile was stiff, barely reaching her eyes; stabbed by a deep unease, he said without finesse, "Years ago, when you were too young to know the difference, Raoul and Lucie put you in a cage. But now you know where the key is."

"You're the key," she said tonelessly, "that's what you mean, isn't it?"

He nodded. "Have any of your other men met your parents?"

"Of course not."

"I rest my case," Slade said. "And now, much as I don't want to, I've got to go." He bent his head, kissing her with all the confusion of emotion she aroused in him just by existing, feeling her resistance. Against her lips, her delectably soft lips, he said roughly, "That day in Belle's garden, it was as though something in me recognized you. Desire calling to desire…a force of nature."

His kiss and his words seared through Clea's flesh, all the way to her soul. Panic-stricken, she mumbled, "I hope you'll be able to straighten things out in Oslo."

The challenge wasn't Oslo, Slade thought. The challenge was Clea, so desirable and so elusive. He pulled her the length of his body, holding her with all his strength, then releasing her with a reluctance that shuddered through his frame. Turning on his heel, he strode into the customs area. The doors closed behind him.

Was he man enough to meet that challenge?

CHAPTER TEN

FOUR days after leaving Clea in the airport at Lexington, Slade was stepping out of the shower in his hotel suite in Oslo. It was a marble shower with multiple jets. The water had pummeled some of the exhaustion from his muscles; anticipation would do the rest.

He'd worked day and night, calling on all his formidable skills of negotiation and his iron will, and he'd won. One more chain of environmentally sound paper mills in the world.

He liked winning, he thought, scrubbing himself with the luxuriously thick towel. But now it was time to switch gears, to call on other skills which weren't nearly as well honed. It was time to meet Clea, and win her.

He'd find out where she was from Bill. Some alpine skiing would suit him just fine.

Clea in his bed would suit him better. Despite his single-minded focus the last four days, she'd never been far from his thoughts, and as always had tormented his sleep.

From Manhattan, Bill relayed the information that two days ago Clea hadn't been sure if she'd stay in St. Moritz or head for Chamonix; she hadn't been in touch since then.

His jaw set, the towel cinched around his waist, Slade made half a dozen quick phone calls, ascertaining that Clea had been staying in a chalet in Chamonix the last couple of nights.

She hadn't bothered letting him know where she was.

Anger bit through anticipation. He was through playing games. He was going to Chamonix and he was going to bed Clea. In bed, with her naked beside him, he'd bring her face-to-face with the woman she was meant to be—passionate and passionately generous—trusting the consequences to luck and his own skills of persuasion.

If he could enforce his will on a boardroom of obdurate businessmen, he could surely handle one red-haired woman.

Slade arrived in the French town of Chamonix well after midnight. Early the next morning, he stationed himself near the base of the cable car, enjoying what must be one of the most spectacular views in Europe as he waited for Clea to appear.

In front of him Mont Blanc pierced a sky that was a dazzling blue. Snow, rock, the dark green of fir trees, the serried peaks of Les Grands Montets: no claustrophobia here, he thought. Not even a whiff of it.

He was in ski gear, goggles looped around his neck. He could have walked to the small private chalet where Clea was staying; but from his contact in Chamonix he'd discovered that she'd skied early the last two mornings, either alone or with a guide, so he'd decided to wait for her outdoors.

He was going skiing with her, whether she wanted him to or not. It was all part of his campaign.

And then he saw her, walking toward him in a slim-fitting yellow suit, her hair pulled back, dark glasses perched on her nose. She was carrying skis and poles over one shoulder. She could have been wrapped in a tarp, he thought, and he'd still have known her; his heart was thumping in his chest as though he'd just run the moguls half a mile from here.

A man in blue racing gear came out of a building advertising instructors and guides. Hailing her, he kissed her on both cheeks with a familiarity that made Slade's hackles rise. After they'd talked for several minutes, the man went back inside, the sun slanting across his thatch of blond hair. Clea kept walking, the smile still on her face.

Slade stepped onto the road. "Good morning, Clea."

She stopped as if she'd been shot, as if the breath had been slammed from her body. Very slowly, she reached up and took off her dark glasses. "Slade," she said. "Your assistant didn't think you'd be leaving Oslo until tomorrow."

It was information that had been true enough at the time. "I wrapped everything up last night," Slade said.

She needed time to catch her breath. "Successfully, I hope?"

"Very. Were you planning to let me know where you were?"

"Later on today." As he raised one brow derisively, she snapped, "It's true. Not that I needed to bother—you found me anyway." Why was she behaving like a shrew, she thought despairingly, when the sight of him had filled her with a wild torrent of joy?

Why was he making no move to kiss her?

"Where are you skiing this morning?" he demanded.

"Off-piste," she said briefly. "To get away from the crowds."

"Suits me fine."

Her voice was sharp as the ridges on the mountain. "So you're skiing with me?"

"That's the plan."

"You don't look overjoyed at the prospect."

"Looks can be deceiving." He reached out, tracing the line of her cheekbone with one finger. "You haven't been sleeping well. Why not, Clea?"

"The latest downturn in the stock market?" she retorted,

yanking her head away from his touch. "So *are* you overjoyed to see me, Slade?"

His laugh was devoid of amusement. "I never know what I'm feeling when I'm anywhere near you. Although it sure isn't indifference."

"Is that supposed to be a compliment?"

"Whatever you feel for me, Clea, it isn't indifference either," he said softly. "Are we going skiing or are we going to stand here half the morning exchanging brilliant repartee?"

"It's not brilliant, it's stupid," she said irritably, "and I truly was going to let Bill know that I was in Chamonix."

Her eyes were flaring with emotions Slade couldn't have named to save his soul. "Okay, I believe you," he said, and cupped her face in his palms, feeling the early morning chill on her cheeks. His voice roughened. "Maybe all along I've been in as much of a cage as you have—all those carefully orchestrated affairs I had, and the distance I kept between myself and my emotions. But it's too easy to stay locked up, Clea, everything safe and under control. You and I mean something to each other, I swear we do. Whatever's between us, it matters."

Staring down at her shiny white-and-yellow ski boots, Clea said rapidly, "I think about you all the time, I'm awake half the night every night, and food is the last thing on my list. But it's not because I'm in love with you—it's because I'm afraid."

"It's yourself you're afraid of, not me," Slade said bluntly.

"Maybe. Maybe not." She moved her shoulders restlessly. "Who are you afraid of? You? Me? An avalanche?"

"You have the knack of asking unanswerable questions," he said. "How about all three? And now let's go skiing."

"Okay," she said, gave him a rueful smile and headed for the cable car.

Using their passes, they got on the car that would carry them up eight thousand meters to the top of Les Grands

Montets. Slade was blind to the scenery; he hadn't really got used to the simple fact of Clea's presence at his side. Was he in danger of falling in love with her?

Another unanswerable question.

They said almost nothing to each other on the ascent; the car was crowded and Slade wasn't in the mood for chitchat. After they'd disembarked and were clipping on their skis, Clea asked with impersonal briskness, "Do you know the territory?"

He shook his head. "Then you'd better hang close," she said. "This is no place to get lost—glaciers, crevasses, rock outcrops, and after a while they all look identical. Ready?"

She was adjusting her goggles. Slade did the same, feeling a rush of adrenaline at the prospect of steep slopes and deep, powdery snow. Coupled with a cloudless sky, it was an unbeatable combination.

Well, not really. He and Clea in bed together would be the ultimate unbeatable combination.

She pushed off, her skis carving graceful S's down the fall line as she gathered speed. They stayed on the trail for the first few hundred meters. But then she took a sharp turn to the left, kicking up a spray of fine, dry snow. Virgin snow, Slade noticed, with another rush of adrenaline. He was, quite literally, putting his life in her hands. He knew it, and so, he was sure, did she.

As the couloir opened up, he accelerated to join her, their skis leaving a series of wide, snakelike curves. Pushing in his heels at the turns, flexing his legs to keep his skis from sinking, Slade was filled with an exhilarating sensation of floating, weightless, over the snow, and was filled, too, with a deep certainty. He was going to win Clea if it was the last thing he did.

They skirted a deep bowl, then plunged down another corridor. Her arms relaxed, knees flexed, Clea jumped over a rock outcrop, landing so smoothly that Slade laughed out loud and took the same jump, the wind flattening his jacket to his chest, his knees absorbing the impact.

They were alone with the mountains and the sky.

Of course he was going to win her, he thought exultantly. What other ending could a day such as this have? Wasn't that why he'd wanted to go skiing in the first place?

On her next jump, Clea did a spread-eagle, then swirled to a halt. Not to be outdone, Slade did a variation on the mule-kick, watching her wave her pole in acknowledgment, her teeth gleaming white in a wide grin.

Like all good things, their solitude had to end. Ten minutes later they rejoined the piste, with its neat signposts and small clusters of skiers. Tucking her poles under her arms, Clea schussed down the slope, coming out of it in a spray of snow near the tree line. More decorously, she continued her descent to the bottom of the trail, where she came to a dramatic stop in another swirl of snow.

Slade pulled up beside her and shoved his goggles up on his forehead. "Fantastic!" he said, laughing for sheer pleasure from that wild descent.

She was laughing, too, her cheeks pink from the wind, her eyes as brilliant as sky and snow. "I can't really compliment you for being a mean skier, because I was nearly always ahead of you."

"I was an idiot to ever call you a coward," he said, put his arms around her, pulled her close and kissed her with all the reckless passion with which they'd skied. She strained her body to his, her lips parting, her tongue darting to find his. Slade said thickly, "My hotel's right across the street."

"Let's go," she said, leaning into him as he put one arm around her waist.

Outside the ultramodern hotel, they locked their skis and poles in the racks. In the lobby they headed for the stairs, walking side by side, Slade aware of Clea through every pore in his body. She was yanking off her toque, shaking her hair free in a glorious mass of curls. They took the stairs at a run, hampered by their boots, and within moments Slade was ushering her into his suite.

He locked the door and pulled her toward him, finding her mouth with his, drinking deep of her sweetness. "Your lips are cold," he muttered. "You're all I want, all I ever wanted—come to bed with me."

"Yes," she said, yanking the zipper down on her jacket. Her white sweater clung to her breasts; she was still breathing hard. Bending down, she started to unclasp her boots.

Slade kicked his own boots aside and stripped off his jacket. Clea, he noticed, his breath catching in his throat, was stepping out of her yellow trousers and pulling her tights down her legs. Quickly her turtleneck and synthetic T-shirt followed the tights. "Clea," he said hoarsely.

Now was the time to unlock the cage, she thought. Now, with Slade, the one man who was the key. She said with a daredevil tilt of her chin, "You're letting me get ahead of you again."

Her sports underwear couldn't really be called sexy. But had he ever seen anything more beautiful than the woman leaning against the wall as she pulled off her socks? He hauled his sweater over his head, the air cool on his bare flesh, and dropped his ski pants to the floor. Then he jammed her against the wall, kissing her until he thought he'd die from pleasure and unassuaged desire.

Her hands were frantically exploring his chest, his shoulders, the bone of rib cage and muscle of belly. His erection was instant and fierce; when she pushed herself hard against him, his heart felt as though it was trying to hammer its way out of his chest.

Her hips writhing of their own accord, Clea gasped, "I've dreamed about this—"

"Me, too." He kissed her more deeply, his tongue caught between her teeth. With one hand he found the swell of her breast, teasing the nipple beneath the soft fabric of her bra. She pulled back and in a swift movement drew the bra over her head, throwing it to the floor; her breasts, full and rose-tipped, gleamed softly in the morning light.

Slade lowered his head, tracing the rise of her flesh with his tongue, taking her nipple and suckling her as she moaned his name over and over again, her hair rippling to her shoulders in a dance of fire, her body arched. And all the while she was thrusting her hips against his.

He pulled her underwear down her thighs, and hastily she stepped out of them. "Your turn," she said thickly, reaching for his waistband. Moments later her body was pressed to his, naked, warm and infinitely desirable. He was losing control, Slade thought dimly, everything vanishing but the imperative need to enter her. "The bed," he muttered against her mouth.

She seized his hand and drew it down her belly to the juncture of her thighs, to the wet heat that told him how ready she was. "Touch me," she whispered, losing the last remnants of shyness. "Oh, Slade, I want you, I want you."

Stroking her, his own body drumming in response to hers, he drew back, watching the storm gather in her face. She gave a sharp cry, her slender frame shuddering and trembling, her breathing frantic as a trapped bird's. And still he stroked her, eliciting from her a passion that excited him beyond belief.

She was whimpering now, faster and faster, until she broke against him with one last cry of repletion. He pulled her close, feeling the pounding of her heart like his own. But as he went to lift her in his arms, Clea looped her thighs around his waist and drew his head down to kiss her once again, her features still dazzled with surrender.

He couldn't wait; it would be more than anyone could ask of him. Hard and sure, Slade drove into her, watching her face convulse with reawakened longing. Slick, hot, welcoming, she took him in. And he was lost.

From a long way away, he heard his voice cry out her name and hers answer him, urgent, imperative. Her body's inner throbbing seized him, inflaming his own rhythms until, in a convulsion of need he couldn't have withstood, he emptied himself deep within her. Burying his face in her bare shoulder, he held her tight, never wanting to let her go, wishing this moment could last forever.

Her hair smelled sweetly of flowers; her skin was damp with sweat. Drinking in every sensation, Slade for the first time in his life knew what it meant to become one flesh. Old-fashioned words, he thought. But hadn't making love with Clea banished any boundaries between her body and his? Linked her to him even more strongly?

"Slade, Slade," Clea muttered, feeling as though she'd just fallen over a precipice. "I've never…I mean, that was so—"

"Fast," he supplied, looking up with the faintest of smiles, his chest still heaving.

Her cheeks were suffused with pink. "Was it too fast? I should have—"

"Two of us are involved here, so let's leave *should* out of the equation. Anyway, we're going to do it differently next time. Properly. Taking our time."

Her flush deepened. "There's nothing remotely proper about making love against a wall. I can't believe I did that."

"I can. And being improper with you…what better way to spend the day?"

"So we're going to do it again?" she said saucily.

He ran his lips down the taut line of her throat, feeling her tremble to his touch. "I think we should," he said.

She chuckled deep in her throat. "That kind of *should* I can deal with." Then her smile faded. "I've only just started taking the pill," she blurted. "The doctor thought it might help with the cramps I have every month—I told him how I'd fainted. But I don't know if the pills have kicked in yet."

So she hadn't been on the pill prior to meeting him; wasn't that one more clue that she wasn't nearly as promiscuous as she'd indicated? Slade said flatly, "I always use protection anyway. But it never entered my mind."

"Or mine."

Shifting her in his arms, Slade carried her through into his bedroom, which overlooked a range of startlingly white peaks etched against a blue sky. He put her down on the bed and rested his body on top of hers, his weight pressing her into the mattress. "This time we'll remember," he said. "Because this time we won't rush—we have all the time in the world."

In the turquoise depths of her eyes he saw the stirrings of panic coupled with desire. Leaning down, he kissed her forehead, her cheekbones, the spun silk of her hair; panic was his enemy, he knew that. "You're so beautiful, so soft and warm, so unbelievably sexy…your skin smells of lilacs."

"Soap," she said, her eyes drifting shut as he continued his exploration, nibbling at her lips, parting them with his tongue, kissing her with all tenderness welling within him.

Tenderness. Another new emotion.

"Your eyes remind me of the sea," he said, "your hair's like embers."

"You could write a Shakespearean sonnet," Clea murmured, her heart melting within her. "You say such lovely things to me."

"It's not difficult. In fact, it's superlatively easy. Although maybe we could leave the sonnet for another time."

She smiled, taking his face in her hands and kissing him almost shyly; oddly, she felt as though this was the first time they'd really been together. He took his cue from her, easing down to lie beside her so he could slowly move the length of her body. Exploring as he went, playing on all her sensitivities, he exulted in the eagerness with which she met him, and in the little starbursts of surprise that overtook her, but most of all in the wonderment that suffused her flushed features.

Wonderment, he thought. As if making love with him was giving her far more than she'd anticipated or imagined.

He pushed the thought aside to feast on every inch of her, feeling tension gather in muscle and sinew, hearing her tiny moans of pleasure, her whispered requests, each punctuated by small, frantic kisses. "Oh, yes, Slade…oh, again. Again."

And all the while, her hands were smoothing his shoulders, wandering over his torso and hip bones. She tangled her fingers in the dark hair on his chest, tugging gently, and with her lips traced collarbone, breastbone and ribs; her cheek was resting over his heart, with its imperious tattoo.

It was like a dream, Slade thought, and yet simultaneously more real than anything he'd ever done before. The woman he'd desired for months was in his arms. In his bed. What more could he ask?

With a gentleness that disarmed him, her hands drifted lower, delicately encircling him. "So silky, so hard," she marveled, her eyes trained to his face, her blood thrumming in her veins. "You like me doing that."

"God, yes," he groaned. Then, as she lifted herself to straddle him, he quickly dealt with the protection he'd earlier put on the bedside table, and slid inside her. With the same exquisite, agonizing delicacy, she rode him, up and down, side to side, overwhelming him with the sweet ache of longing and the fierce impulsions of his own blood.

Rolling sideways, carrying her with him, he buried his face in the soft valley between her breasts. "Stop," he muttered, "or I won't be able to—"

"Do you have any idea how that makes me feel?" she said. "Where did I get so much power?"

He could have joked. He could have called her a sexy chick and made her giggle again. He could simply have kept quiet, kissing her into another of those tranced silences. Instead Slade said, his breath wafting over her skin, "I'm so happy to be here with you, Clea. Happier than I thought possible."

A tiny shudder rippled through her body; and he knew it for a resurgence of fear, not delight. Dammit, he thought, you're not going to be afraid of me or of my feelings. I'm not going to give you the chance.

Taking her nipple in his mouth, he tugged at it, feeling it tighten like a pebble on the beach. As her heart began to race beneath his fingertips, he stroked her other breast with hypnotic slowness until her tiny cries of delight danced in the air. Only then did he wrap his thighs around hers and touch the wet petals of her flesh, hearing her gasp, feeling her body buck and arch. Her climax ripped through her, her single sharp cry echoing in his ears.

Clea collapsed into him, boneless in surrender, hearing her own breathing ragged against his shoulder. "You did it again," she gasped.

"We're not done yet," he said, smiling into her eyes as he lifted himself on his elbows, his big body hovering over her. Very slowly he again eased inside her.

Her eyes widened. "I still want you," she whispered, awestruck. "How can I?"

"Because I'm irresistible," he teased. His voice deepened. "Because you're passionate, more passionate than I could have imagined. And believe me, Clea, where you and bed are concerned, my imagination's been working overtime."

"You talk too much," she said spiritedly, and suddenly thrust against him, again and again, her irises darkening, her hair spread like a silken fan on the pillow.

The fire caught him in its heat and willingly he entered it. Crushing her breasts against his chest, he moved with her, two rhythms as one, falling into the flames, falling as one, falling and falling…and distantly heard his own hoarse cry of satiation.

Beyond words, almost beyond feelings, Slade rolled over to lie beside her, enfolding her in his embrace. "You've done me in," he muttered.

Gently as the brush of a bird's wing, Clea kissed him on the mouth. "It's mutual," she whispered, and felt her lashes drifting down, her body languorous with the need to sleep.

The image was imprinted on Slade's brain: Clea, her hair tumbling over his bare shoulder, her lips swollen from his kisses, falling asleep. Then he, too, closed his eyes and slept.

Although the sun had fallen behind the mountains, it was still daylight. What was he doing in bed?

Slade reared up on one elbow. He was alone in the bed. "Clea!" he called. "Where are you?"

But somehow he knew, even before he opened his mouth, that he was the only one in his suite. As he put his feet to the floor, the first thing he saw was a folded piece of hotel stationery lying on the bedside table. His name was scrawled on the outside.

His heart cold as a glacier, he picked up the paper and flattened it on his knee. "Slade," he read, "I lose myself when I'm with you, I don't know who I am anymore. I have to be alone so I can think this through. I'll be in touch, I promise. But please don't follow me."

The writing was agitated. There was no signature.

He didn't need a signature.

She'd gone. But when? His gaze fell on the digital clock, also on the bedside table. Five-thirty, he thought in dismay. How could he have slept so long?

Easily. Because he'd been sleep-deprived for days, and he'd just made impassioned love with the woman he'd wanted more than any other woman in the world.

Buck-naked, Slade strode into the next room. All Clea's clothes were gone. The scent of lilacs lingered in the air.

With a muttered curse Slade headed for the bathroom. Moving fast, he showered, dressed and packed up his gear. Then, doing up his jacket as he went, he hurried downstairs.

Her chalet wasn't far from his hotel. But when he stopped outside a charming wooden building enclosed in evergreens, its balcony facing the mountains, he knew intuitively that it was empty. He banged on the door, unsurprised when he got no response.

Again going on intuition, he walked to the guide office and stepped inside. Giving the receptionist his best smile, he said in French, "I'm looking for a blond-haired man in a blue ski suit...a friend of Clea Chardin's."

"Lothar Hesse. He's our best guide and instructor."

"Is he around?"

"No. He and Clea left together, actually, a couple of hours ago. They were driving to the airport at Geneva."

"I'm sorry to have missed them," Slade said through a red haze of fury and jealousy. "Do you know where they were going?"

"Lothar had plans to fly to Hamburg. Ardlaufen, his home town, is only ten miles outside the city." She lowered her voice conspiratorially. "Clea and Lothar were a very hot item a couple of years ago, so I wouldn't be surprised if they've gone to Ardlaufen together. Lothar has the next two days off, and there's a lot more privacy there than in Chamonix."

His jaw clenched, Slade said, "He'll be back in a couple of days, then?"

"Oh, yes, he's very reliable." The receptionist pouted. "I wouldn't mind being in Ardlaufen with him, he's such a hunk and a sweetheart into the bargain. But what chance have I got against someone like Clea Chardin? Beautiful and rich. Some people have all the luck."

Managing another smile, Slade said, "Thanks for your help," and walked outside again.

Fifteen minutes later he was on the road to Geneva. With him traveled demons of doubt, demons Clea herself had planted over the weeks since they'd met. Was she incapable of fidelity, as she'd suggested? Had she gone right from his bed to Lothar's?

She couldn't have. Not Clea. No, their lovemaking had indeed turned her world upside down, forcing her to confront her own passionate nature. Guarded and defensive as she was—and who knew that better than he?—she'd run away from her new knowledge, and from him. Opportunely Lothar, an old friend, had offered her a drive.

Being in bed with Clea had turned his own world upside down, opening a floodgate of emotions new to him. Clea, more vulnerable, must have found it devastating to her carefully constructed image of herself. Of course she'd fled for cover.

Please don't follow me…

He had to. What other choice was there?

CHAPTER ELEVEN

Taking out his cell phone, Slade got the number of a private investigator from his contact in Chamonix, phoned him and gave him some terse instructions. Within fifteen minutes he had his answer. Clea and Lothar were on their way to Hamburg. Clea had booked her passage at the airport. Lothar, on the other hand, had purchased his ticket two weeks ago.

Choosing to be encouraged by this, for it meant their traveling together hadn't been premeditated, Slade drove on. The investigator had stationed someone at the arrivals terminal in Hamburg. So once he, Slade, arrived in Hamburg, he would know where Lothar and Clea had gone.

Please don't follow me.

You're not running away from me, he thought. I saw your face in the moment of climax, I watched your every reaction. And I'd swear that in bed with me you found a woman new to you. A woman whose existence you'd scarcely guessed… that's who you're running from.

If he was wrong, then what?

He wasn't wrong. Clea's shyness, the wonderment rising in her face like the morning sun, her unbridled passion, all of them cried out to him that he was right.

Hold that hope, he thought grimly. And he was still holding

it at dusk, when he finally arrived in Hamburg. There he found out that Lothar and Clea had driven to Ardlaufen in Lothar's blue Volkswagen. They'd gone to a restaurant for dinner, and were on their way to a nightclub on Günter Strasse.

Slade picked up yet another rental car, checked a local map and left the airport. Ardlaufen was a pretty little town on the Elbe, its streets lined with tall gabled houses and neatly trimmed evergreens. The nightclub was, Slade discovered, on the ground floor of an old warehouse; among the cars parked along the curb was a blue Volkswagen.

He got out of his own car, stretching his shoulders. The day felt as though it had gone on forever, from early this morning when he'd stationed himself by a ski lift in Chamonix to now, when he was standing outside a nightclub in a small town in northern Germany.

Taking a deep breath, Slade walked into the club.

Swiftly his eyes adjusted to the gloom. Too swiftly, because he saw Clea right away. She and Lothar were dancing to a slow and lazily sensual blues rhythm, his arms around her waist, hers around his neck, her face pressed to his shoulder. His head was downbent, his lips against her hair.

They were totally absorbed in each other.

The knife that stabbed Slade to the heart went far beyond jealousy to an agony he'd never experienced before. He blundered out of the club, dimly aware that the bouncer was watching him in surprise, and found himself outside on the brick walk. His lungs heaving, he drew in great gulps of air, desperate to loosen the terrible constriction in his chest.

Once, in university, as a novice boxer, he'd been hit by a pro. He had the same sensation now of gut-wrenching violence and total disorientation. The primly decorated houses swayed on their foundations. The stars dipped and shimmered, and the clipped branches of the trees whirled in front of his eyes.

Slowly, painfully, through a storm of emotion, a single fact confronted him. All along, Clea had been telling him the truth. She *was* incapable of fidelity. She did go from man to man, from bed to bed.

From him to Lothar in less than twelve hours. The evidence had been seared into his brain only moments ago. Unarguable. Ineradicable.

It took Slade three tries to unlock his car door. Carefully he eased into the seat and pulled the door shut. Then he sat very still, concentrating on his breathing.

Gradually the world righted itself. The trees were simply trees, their boughs without movement on this windless night. The stars stayed in their appointed orbits, glimmering coldly, speaking of distances beyond imagining, and of incredible loneliness.

Clea was like her mother: the cure for any difficulty was to change men. The only difference being, as Lucie had said, that Clea didn't bother marrying them.

She'd fooled him from beginning to end. Or had he, all too willingly, allowed himself to be fooled? Because, of course, he'd learned something else the last ten minutes. Something just as devastating. He was in love with Clea.

He loved her wholly, desperately and irrevocably. Had for weeks, probably, disguising it behind words like *sex* and *desire*.

How stupid could he be, he thought with brutal truth. For a man known for acuity, he'd been unbelievably obtuse. He not only hadn't realized he was falling in love; he'd done so with a woman who'd left his bed for another man's within a matter of hours.

At least she didn't know he loved her.

His secret.

Pain slammed through him, and momentarily he dropped his forehead to the wheel. His secret and his burden.

How the gods must be laughing. He'd fallen in love, finally, with a woman incapable of loving him back. Beguiled by her beauty and her intelligence, he'd made the worst mistake in his life.

He had no idea how to undo that mistake.

How did you fall out of love?

Slade was no nearer a solution to that dilemma a few days later when he pulled up outside Belle Hayward's Victorian mansion in San Francisco. He was on his way home from trade shows in Vietnam, South Korea and China. Had he been in the best of spirits it would have been an exhausting trip. As it was, he felt far beyond exhaustion. Numbness was what he was seeking, and that was what he'd achieved.

He'd dropped Clea from his life as if she'd never been part of it, making no move to find out where she was or who she was with. The first thing he'd done after leaving Ardlaufen was to leave a message with his assistant, Bill: if Clea contacted him, she was to be told that Slade was permanently unavailable.

Please don't follow me. How ironic a request, given the circumstances.

He still hadn't come to terms with how awry his judgment of Clea had been from beginning to end. Sometimes a lightning bolt of denial would shoot through him: Clea was innocent of wrongdoing, had been honest with him all along. At times like this, he'd reach for the phone, desperate to locate her. But then, inevitably, the image that had burned into his brain in the nightclub in Ardlaufen would confront him once again, and hope would drown in a bitter sea of regret.

He loathed this seesawing of his emotions, with its plunges into denial, hope and despair. He also hated his own self-doubt; he'd always prided himself on knowing his own mind and the minds of others.

Not anymore.

Was he going to sit here all afternoon staring at Belle's front door? Or was he going in to say hello? His flight east didn't leave until tomorrow, because he'd learned from hard experience to take a day's break when the jet lag was so extreme. So he certainly had time for a visit.

What was he, a man or a mouse? So what if Belle knew Clea? So what if he himself had gate-crashed Belle's dinner with Clea last October, and had ended up driving Clea from this very house back to her hotel? He wasn't going to cut Belle out of his life on Clea's account. Belle had been a friend for too long to do that.

He got out of the car, marched up the steps and pressed the bell. Within moments the door was opened by the butler. "Hello, Carter," Slade said. "Is Mrs. Hayward in?"

"Come this way, sir."

Slade was ushered into the formal parlor, where the stag's head sneered at him from over the mantel. His gaze winced away from the dark little oil painting of the man in shackles being led into the cave. Self-portrait, he thought, and passionately wished he'd gotten on the first flight east.

"Slade," Belle cried, walking in the room and giving him a quick hug. She was wearing purple pants with a bright yellow top, her gray hair fluffy as a seed head.

"Hello, Belle," Slade said with genuine affection, kissing her cheek. "How are you?"

"Have you come to see Clea?"

The muscles in his face froze. "Clea?" he repeated stupidly.

"She's at the site right now, but she's staying here. You should join us for tea—she'll be home by three-thirty."

"Site? What site?"

Belle said sharply, "Didn't you know she's here? Have I put my foot in it again? It does seem to be a talent of mine. One of the few that's expanding with age—like my waistline," she finished gloomily.

Slade said flatly, "No, I didn't know Clea was here. I came to see you."

"Oh," said Belle. "Then I've put both feet in it."

"What's she doing here?" he snarled.

Belle put her head to one side, assessing him. "The two of you look like half-starved insomniacs," she announced. "Clea clams up if I as much as mention your name, and you obviously had no idea of her whereabouts. Yet it's as plain as the diamonds on my fingers that you're in love with each other. I just wish you'd get on with it."

"She's not the slightest bit in love with—"

"Do you know where Rosa Street is?"

"No. She's not—"

"I'll get the map. You stay right here." And Belle bustled out of the room.

He was thirty-five years old. Was he going to allow Mrs. Henry Hayward III to boss him around as if he were six? Slade strode out into the hall just as Belle reappeared holding a San Francisco street map. He said brusquely, "If Clea's staying with you, I'm out of here."

"This is how you get to Rosa Street. You'll find her at a building site on the corner of Rosa and Ventley. The rest is up to you."

Slade stared at the map. "What kind of building site?"

"You'll see." Unexpectedly Belle put her hand on his sleeve. "I try very hard not to ask anything of the younger generation. But I'm going to break my own rule. Go and see her, Slade. Please."

Belle disliked displays of emotion. He said, "Clea and I

went to bed together in Chamonix. Then she ran away with another man. I'm sure you've heard of her reputation—believe me, it's earned."

"Are you telling me she's promiscuous?"

"I'm telling you she wasn't faithful to me for the space of a single day."

"I don't believe it."

"Belle, I saw her," he said harshly. "She ran away with a ski instructor she had an affair with a couple of years ago."

"It can't be true." Belle's bosom swelled indignantly. "There's got to be an explanation." Then she frowned at him, her eyes narrowing. "Anyway, what do you care? She's just another woman. Dump her."

"I've fallen in love with her."

"In love? *You?*"

"Yeah." His smile was wintry. "Serves me right—is that what you're thinking?"

"Give me a little more credit than that. Go to the building site, Slade. Ask her about the ski instructor. Because if she's promiscuous, I'm—I'm—"

She was flapping her arms, at a loss for words. "A lousy judge of character," Slade supplied dryly.

"She's a good woman. I'd stake my fortune on it."

Belle had always had the knack for seeing through any pretensions to the real person. Deep within him he felt, once again, the agonizing stirrings of hope. "All right," he heard himself say, "I'll drive to Rosa Street."

"Off you go, then."

Nearly forty minutes later Slade pulled up near the junction of Rosa and Ventley. A two-story building was going up on the north corner, an institution of some kind, judging by the window placement and the wide entranceway. A small crane pivoted serenely over the roof, scaffolding scaled the walls and a cement truck was parked on the street. Workers were visible on both floors, wearing jackets against the cool air.

A man holding a sheaf of blueprints came out of the front door. Clea was walking at his side. She was wearing overalls, her vivid red hair tucked under a yellow hard hat. She and the contractor stood on the sidewalk having an animated discussion, Clea gesturing at the second floor, the contractor nodding every now and then.

A couple of the workers joined them on the pavement. Clea said something to them, and they laughed.

What the hell was going on?

She and the contractor shook hands. Then Clea headed across the sidewalk toward a small green car. Slade got out of his own vehicle and crossed the street. She was tossing her hard hat in the backseat when he came up behind her. "Hello, Clea," he said.

She jumped as if he'd dropped a brick through her windshield. Whirling, she gasped, "*Slade!* What are you doing here?"

"I could ask the same of you."

Shock was instantly routed by rage. So angry she could hardly talk, she spat, "It didn't take you long to disappear after Chamonix. I phoned your office to tell you where I was and was given—oh, ever so politely—the brush-off. *I'm sorry to tell you Mr. Carruthers is no longer available.*" Her voice rose. "Thanks, Slade. Thanks a lot."

"Quit playing games, Clea! There was a damn good reason I cut you out of my life."

"Yes, there was," she seethed. "You got what you wanted. Me in bed. Game over."

"That's not true and you know it," he blazed. "Tell me—how's Lothar?"

"Lothar?" She blinked. "As far as I know, he's fine...but what's he got to do with it?"

Slade took her by the arm, his fingers digging into her flesh. "You went straight from my bed to his. How could you do that, Clea? How *could* you?"

Her jaw dropped. "You're saying I went to bed with *Lothar?*"

"Don't play the innocent—we're way past that."

"We sure are! Let go—you're hurting my arm."

"I'm not letting go until I've gotten a few answers. Truthful ones, for once—if you're capable of them."

"You told me I could trust you," she fumed. "That you wouldn't dump me, you'd—"

"Trouble here, Clea?"

Slade turned his head, still gripping Clea by the arm. The contractor and two of the workers had gathered on the side-walk, all three of them assessing him warily. "No," Slade snapped.

"Yes," said Clea.

"The only trouble she's in is that the past has caught up with her," Slade grated. "I want answers and I'm going to get them. So you guys can butt out."

The contractor said easily, "You want us to leave, Clea?"

She shot Slade a hostile glance. "Maybe not. Although—"

"Let's start right here," Slade rasped, glaring at the con-tractor. "What the devil's this building and what's her connec-tion with it?"

"It's a school for disadvantaged kids," he said. "Street kids. Reformed druggies. Clea's paying for it, along with Mrs. Hayward."

Slade looked straight at Clea. "Is that true?"

"Yes."

His brain made a lightning-swift connection. "You do this in Europe, too, don't you? Those kids we met at Tivoli—were they in one of your schools?" Again she nodded. "Why didn't you tell me?" he lashed.

"I don't talk about it. To the press. To my friends. Certainly not to my parents."

"Or to me." It was odd, he thought distantly, that she still had the power to hurt him.

"I didn't know you well enough."

"You knew me well enough to get in bed with me."

"The worst mistake I ever made!"

"It didn't take you long to get over it. With Lothar." He turned to the contractor. "I've fallen in love with this woman. Which is the dumbest move I—"

"You're not in love with me!" Clea gasped, her brain whirling.

"Yes, I am." Again he addressed the contractor. "Clea might have more money than she knows what to do with, but she comes from a lousy background. Instead of looking after her own needs, though, she builds schools like this for troubled kids. Very admirable of her. But until she comes to terms with her own family, it doesn't do her—or me—a pick of good."

"Be quiet, Slade—I hate the way you're talking about me as if I don't exist."

"I followed you to Ardlaufen," he grated. "I saw you and Lothar on the dance floor of that nightclub, wrapped around each other like a couple of mating seals. You and I made love, Clea—that very day. Or at least, I made love. There are other words for what you did."

She said carefully, "You saw me and Lothar in the nightclub?"

"Congratulations—you're finally getting the message."

"I've never gone to bed with Lothar," she said with fierce emphasis. "He's a friend, a good friend, and that's all."

"That's not what it looked like to me."

She shot a glance over her shoulder at the three men on the sidewalk. "Slade, do we really have to discuss all these intimate details in front of an audience?"

"Yep," said the contractor. "He's a big guy, Clea, and plenty mad. We'll just hang around till we see how it shakes."

"Okay, Slade Carruthers," Clea announced, "you asked for it. I ran away from you in Chamonix. I'm not going to apologize for that—you turned my world upside down and scared me half to death. Lothar was going home for the weekend, so I went with him. What you saw in the nightclub was him comforting me after I'd spent the better part of two hours weeping on his shoulder…because I was so unhappy. Because I didn't see how I could stay with you, and yet I couldn't bear leaving you."

He stared at her in silence. The breeze was whipping her hair around her head. Her eyes blazed with honesty. He said, "You had your arms around his neck."

"I was exhausted," she snapped. "I'd have fallen down if he hadn't been holding me up. I knew if I stayed in that hotel in Chamonix with you, I'd be in danger of falling in love with you. And what then? Marry you? Like my mother marries all the men she falls in love with? Not likely."

"Are you in love with me, Clea?" Slade said urgently.

She ran her fingers through her hair in unconscious drama. "No! Maybe. I don't know. I've never been in love in my life. And once I'd spoken to your assistant, I was so angry I did my best to stop thinking about you altogether."

"Did you succeed?"

She glowered at him; the truth was, she'd failed miserably. "Never you mind."

"Tell me anyway."

She said shrewishly, "I was going to ask Belle tonight if you'd moved on to another woman."

"Oh sure," Slade said, "I've dated nine different women in the last nine days. For Pete's sake, Clea, I'm in love with you—don't you get it?"

By now she'd totally forgotten their audience. "I'd had exactly one lover up until Chamonix," she announced. "At age nineteen I went to bed with an acquaintance of mine because I wanted to find out what sex was all about. I didn't like it very much, the earth very definitely did not move—the bedsprings scarcely moved—and I was never tempted to repeat the experience."

"All those newspaper articles?" Slade flashed.

"You know the media. If I look sideways at a man, I'm sleeping with him. It sells papers."

He'd had exactly the same experience with regard to women. "Lothar's an old friend," he repeated slowly, "and you were crying on his shoulder."

"His girlfriend was arriving from Trieste the next day."

Slade rubbed at the back of his neck where the muscles were as taut as steel. Prior to Chamonix, Clea had had one lover, an inadequate one at that. He remembered their own lovemaking, with her little starts of surprise, her wonderment, her air of awakening in a new place almost as if she were a virgin, and knew she was telling the truth. She'd never been promiscuous. Far from it. She'd been virtually chaste.

"I totally misjudged you," he said painfully. "There's no possible way I can apologize for that."

"I suppose it must have looked pretty convincing," she said grudgingly.

"Yeah…"

She asked the crucial question. "Do you believe me, Slade? Because if you don't, it really is game over."

"Yes," he said quietly, "I believe you."

He glanced over at the three men. The younger of the two workers said raptly, "It's like a soap opera, right here on the sidewalk."

The contractor said with genuine interest, "Is your mother the reason you don't want to get married, Clea?"

Slade said, "Her mother's been married eight times and her father goes through mistresses quicker than you can pour cement. So Clea's decided marriage is the ultimate dirty word."

"You're doing it again," Clea complained. "Speaking for me."

"I've had plenty of time to think about it in the last week," he said grimly.

The worker to their right, a man in his forties, shoved his hard hat back on his head. "I'm happily married to my high school sweetheart. It gets better and better as time goes along. Sure, we have our ups and downs—we've both got minds of our own, and while the kids are great they bring their own problems. But Liz and me? Solid as the foundation of this school."

The contractor grinned. "True Confessions. I've been in love with the same woman for fifteen years. Wouldn't want it any other way." He turned to the younger man at his side. "What about you, Mikey?"

"Divorced," Mikey said.

"Oh well," the contractor said, "two out of three ain't bad."

"Let's make it three out of four, Clea," Slade said, resting his hands on her taut shoulders, and knowing he was taking a monumental step. "The only way you're going to find out I'm in this for the duration is to marry me. Live with me. Have kids and bring them up, give them the love you missed out on. Then maybe, twenty years down the road, you'll realize how happiness and love—the lasting kind of love—go together."

"You guys are ganging up on me," Clea blurted. "Four to one's not fair."

Slade leaned over and kissed the tip of her nose. "Hey, you can handle odds like that."

The contractor said, "You could take on the whole crew, Clea…okay, guys, we'd better get back to work. Or else the boss'll fire us." And he grinned at Clea.

"I'll see you tomorrow," she said. "Eight o'clock."

Mikey rolled his eyes. "Better make it nine."

As Clea scowled at Mikey, Slade said lightly, "Belle's invited us back for tea. You know Belle, she's a stickler for punctuality."

Slade. Bill. Lothar. Mikey. And now tea with Belle. It was all too much. Clea sketched a goodbye salute to the three men and dove into her car. "I'll see you there, Slade," she said, and drove off in a screech of rubber.

Slade got in his own car and followed her back to Belle's. He didn't want to sit in the parlor and decorously drink tea. He wanted to be in bed with Clea. Only then would he believe she was back in his life again.

When she'd tried to contact him after Chamonix, she must have felt utterly betrayed to be told he was no longer available. How the hell was he ever going to make amends?

By the time he was climbing Belle's steps for the second time that day, Clea had vanished inside. Belle herself let him in. "We're in the sunroom," she said.

At least he was spared the parlor. Slade marched into the solarium, with its pleasant bamboo furnishings and drifts of orchids, hibiscus and orange blossoms. Clea, in her overalls, her back to him, was busily deadheading the Christmas cactus.

Belle said, "Ah, here's the tea. Thank you, Marlene. Sit down, Slade, you look about as relaxed as a caged cougar." She picked up the sterling silver teapot. "Clea, you sit down, too."

Clea, to Slade's surprise, did as she was told. Belle went on, "Help yourself to sandwiches. Milk, Slade?"

Slade nodded and swallowed an asparagus sandwich in one gulp. He was hungry, he realized in faint surprise, and took another. When had he last eaten? In mid-Pacific?

Belle said calmly, "By the look of both of you, nothing's been settled. Clea, I first saw Slade as a babe in arms. I know him through and through and I admire him greatly. He's—"

"Belle," Slade said, "be quiet."

"You be quiet," she snorted. "If Slade says he's in love with you, Clea, he is. No ifs, ands or buts—he doesn't do things in half-measures. So quit thinking that the moment you get a runny nose or decide to take a Ph.D. in Aztec mythology, he's going to vanish like your father and all your mother's husbands. He's not."

"That's what he says," Clea admitted reluctantly.

"Then listen to him." Belle waved her sandwich in the air. "Live with him if you're afraid of marriage."

"Either way is a commitment," Clea snapped.

Belle leaned forward. "Your schools are a wonderful gift to the world. But now it's time for you to go back to school. Unlearn the lessons Raoul and Lucie taught you, and learn what Slade can teach you. Build something new that's just for the pair of you."

Clea was frowning at Belle. "How did you get to know me so well?"

"I liked you from the moment you walked in the door last October proposing you build a school on my land on Rosa Street. Otherwise, do you think I'd have allowed you at the garden party without a hat?"

"In trousers, too," Clea said with a small smile.

"Forgive your inner child," Belle said grandly. "Nourish your heart chakra, run with the wolves—this is California, after all. Or just plain rely on your backbone. Of which you have plenty."

Clea was still frowning. "I have to learn to trust it first."

"Exactly," Belle said. "I suggest you go upstairs, pack your bag and go with Slade wherever he's going. At least for tonight—doesn't every journey begin with a single step?" She leaned back in her chair. "I'm spouting clichés and I've said more than enough."

"My turn," Slade said. "I wish you'd told me about the schools, Clea."

"They hit too close to home," she said clumsily, knowing she owed him an explanation. "If I talked about them, I might have to admit that I've always felt like an abandoned child—me, with all my money. Much easier to keep quiet."

It made perfect sense; it also touched him deeply. He took out his cell phone, called his favorite hotel in the city and booked his usual suite for two nights. Then he looked over at Clea. "Come and stay with me," he said.

The moment of choice. Stay or run. She said faintly, "All right, I'll come."

Into the silence, a grandfather clock in the next room chimed the hour.

CHAPTER TWELVE

CLEA scrambled to her feet. "I'll go and pack," she said and hurried from the room.

Belle said determinedly, "What did you find out in Beijing?" and Slade did his best to talk intelligently about something other than Clea. Then she herself was standing in the doorway, wearing her turquoise wool coat and trousers, carrying a small black suitcase.

"I'm ready," she said, her voice sounding almost normal. "We'll take both cars, Belle. That way I can go to the site when I need to."

So it wasn't until the door of the hotel suite closed behind them that Slade was alone with Clea. He said, wanting only to put her at her ease, "Those were very small sandwiches—would you like to go downstairs for something to eat?"

She put down her suitcase and rested her palms on his chest. "I can't promise I'll fall in love with you," she blurted. "Or marry you. But I do promise I won't run away again. And I won't date anyone else."

His vision blurring, Slade said huskily, "Those are huge promises."

Briefly she brushed his lashes with her fingers. "I need you to promise you won't turn me away again. Being given the brush-off by your assistant—I can't tell you how terrible that made me feel." In spite of herself, her voice shook. "Negated. As if I'd never even existed for you."

"Of course I promise. Clea, I'm more sorry than I can say. I should have marched up to you and Lothar in the nightclub and had it out with you. But I was, quite literally, stunned…all I could do was get out as fast as I knew how and cut you out of my life. And whenever I'd find myself hoping—trusting—that you were innocent, the image of the two of you on the dance floor would tell me otherwise."

"That, and the clippings, and all my protestations about going from man to man." She bit her lip. "I did a good job, didn't I? Too good."

"One of the worst things was feeling I couldn't trust my own judgment anymore."

Her brow wrinkled. "But you do love me—you mean that?"

"Today, tomorrow and forever," he said huskily.

"What have I ever done to deserve that kind of love?"

"I'm not sure we have to earn love," he said. "I suspect it's a gift."

As a single tear slid down her cheek, he wiped it away. "Let's go to bed, Clea."

Trust, she thought. "I've missed you terribly, Slade. I've been so confused, it's been awful. At some point you might want to thank Lothar—he's listened to far too much moaning and complaining."

"Next time, I'll hang around and you can introduce me."

Her smile felt almost natural. "It's a deal."

"Shower," Slade said decisively, "then bed." He swept her up in his arms, carrying her into the bathroom. "You've lost weight," he grunted. "I'll feed you strawberries and cream after we make love, would you like that?"

"Providing the lovemaking's very soon," she said. "Wow, what a lot of mirrors."

"The better to see you with, my dear," he smiled and started stripping off his clothes, tossing his shirt and tie on the chair.

Giving way to impulse, Clea flung her arms around him, almost knocking him off balance, and holding him so tightly he could scarcely breathe. "I can't believe I'm here with you…I'm so sorry I ran away, but I didn't know what else to do."

Burying his face in the fragrant mass of her hair, Slade said, "I love you, Clea. I love you."

Wishing she could say those three small words back to him, she begged, "Hold on to me."

One hand in the small of her back, the other at her hips, Slade drew her to the length of his body. "I'm holding the whole world in my arms," he said. "You can trust me, sweetheart. Trust that I'll always be there for you, no matter what."

Trust. That word again. Pulling back a little, Clea lifted her sweater over her head and quoted Belle. "Every journey begins with a single step," she said.

Her lacy bra, cupping the ivory swell of her breasts, made his head swim. "Take off the rest of your clothes…let me see you. All of you."

She stepped back, her eyes trained on his face, and let her trousers slip to her ankles. Her hose were held up by slender garters, also embroidered with lace. Taking her time, she slid her stockings down her legs one by one. Then she unclasped her bra, freeing the soft weight of her breasts, and eased her lace-edged bikini pants from her hips.

She said breathlessly, "When you look at me like that—I dissolve, Slade."

He tossed his socks on the chair, unbuckled his leather belt and threw trousers and briefs after the socks. He was, he knew, only too ready to ravish her. As she reached out and stroked all his hardness, his face convulsed. "I was on a plane most of the night," he muttered. "A shower's a necessity."

She gave a rich chuckle. "In that case, it's going to be the quickest shower on record."

As the hot water pounded his back, Clea ran the soap up and down his chest, her fingers playing with his wet, sleek body hair. Slade dropped his head and took her breast in his mouth, gently tugging at her nipple until she threw back her head with a sharp cry of pleasure. "I want you now," she gasped. "Now..."

"No hurry," he said, and smoothed her hips with leisurely sensuality. "Delayed gratification is good for the character."

In deliberate provocation she covered his face with tiny kisses, then sought his lips, her tongue darting to meet his. "I bet I could change your mind."

Raw hunger engulfed him. He muttered, "I bet you could," and kissed her back.

She was trembling very lightly, her body aching with desire. "I want to be in bed with you," she whispered.

He reached behind and turned off the shower. Then he grabbed two of the big, soft towels from the heated rack, swathing her in one of them, fastening the other around his hips. "There are little drops caught in your hair," he said. "Like mist. Sea mist."

"Could you live by the sea?" Clea asked with sudden intensity.

"Yes," he said, and forbore to add that he could live anywhere with her.

"When my mother and I lived with Pete in British Columbia, I loved waking to the sound of waves on the shore."

An idea blossomed in Slade's mind, along with a hope so powerful that it frightened him. He pushed both aside. "Bed," he said. "Your character is fine as it is."

So they were laughing as they tumbled into the wide bed. Slade opened his arms and Clea slid into their circle so naturally that it took his breath away. "You look as though you've been doing that for years."

"I've had lots of practice—you wouldn't believe the fantasies I've had about you," she said. "X-rated, I might add."

"How about some X-rated reality?" he murmured, and stroked the soft rise of her breast to its tip.

She shivered, her eyes darkening. Gracefully she lifted herself to hover over him, deliberately offering him the freedom of her body. With exquisite care Slade set about giving her all the pleasure he was capable of giving. His hands and mouth teased and roamed from head to toe, and all the while the tension tightened, notch by notch, caress by caress, until she was writhing beneath him, her frantic cries like those of distant shorebirds.

Only then did Slade slide within her. She arched to gather him, bucked and plunged, and the last vestiges of control left him. Riding her fierce rhythms, caught by them, he joined with her, and losing his own freedom, found a greater freedom.

His climax, long and shuddering, left his chest heaving and his body drained. He fell to the mattress, clasping her in his embrace. If his heart beat any harder, he thought dimly, it would burst from his rib cage.

Very gently Clea smoothed his sweat-slick hair from his forehead, her fingers unsteady. Capturing them in his, he brought them to his lips. "Beautiful Clea…"

She spoke the only truth she knew. "You give me more than I dreamed possible."

"Body and soul—that's what I give you. But don't you see what's happening? Everything I give, you're receiving. You're beginning to open your heart as well as your body."

With all her courage, she met his gaze and stated the obvious. "You're changing me."

"You're changing yourself." And then, because the last thing he wanted was to revive all her old fears, he added, "Strawberries and cream? That was the deal, wasn't it?"

"With champagne."

He reached for the phone. "I'll have to put some clothes on."

"But then you'll take them off and come back to bed." She gave him a wicked grin. "Why haven't any of my fantasies included licking champagne from your body?"

"How about me licking whipped cream from your breasts?"

She pulled up the sheets to hide her scarlet cheeks. "I want a couple of French pastries, too. Strictly for eating."

He picked up the phone and punched the numbers for room service. And, later, in the big bed, fantasy and reality blended in a way highly satisfactory to both of them.

Clea was late arriving at the site the next morning.

While Clea was at the construction site, Slade checked out several Web sites, phoned his father and asked some pointed questions about seafront properties, then contacted a number of real estate agents.

When Clea came back, he kissed her as if she'd been gone for three months rather than three hours. This led to a swift and impassioned lovemaking on the carpet. Afterward, lying still, her head on Slade's shoulder, Clea gasped, "I'm glad Mikey can't see us now."

"I'm glad any number of people can't see us."

She burrowed her face deeper into his chest. "You know what? I have fun with you, Slade."

"I aim to please," he said. "If you can get away, we'll fly east tomorrow. There's something I want to show you."

She lifted her head, her hair silky on his bare chest. "Sure, I can go, the school's shaping up beautifully. But what are you going to show me?"

"A surprise." He cupped one ivory-smooth breast in his hand. "No questions allowed."

Distracted, she said, "If we're going to make love again—because I know that gleam in your eye—it's going to be in bed. I've got carpet burn."

"What are we waiting for?" Slade replied, and wondered if this was what a honeymoon was like, this unsettling mixture of laughter, eroticism and overwhelming tenderness.

A honeymoon implied a wedding.

Two days later, Slade and Clea were driving the rocky shoreline of Maine. When they came to a secluded headland, Slade stopped the car near a pair of black iron gates, and unlocked them with the keys he'd picked up at the airport.

The driveway curved through a forest of pine and spruce, the boughs weighted with soft billows of fresh snow; then it opened into a vista of low granite cliffs and boundless sea. The house faced the ocean; built of stone, cedar and glass, it looked steadfast, as though it could withstand any number of storms. As Slade switched off the engine, Clea whispered, "The only thing I can hear is the waves on the shore...what a beautiful place."

"We could buy it," he said, his throat tight. "Use it as our home base."

She was chewing on her lip, her heart racketing around in her chest. "Are you proposing to me?"

"No," he said. "Shared accommodation and our own bed. That's enough for now."

"That's a lot."

"We'd just be taking Belle's advice," he said mildly, watching her like a hawk. "Live together, isn't that what she suggested? Do you want to go inside? I've got the keys."

"I'd love to," Clea said, knowing that once again Slade had thrown her off balance. Live with him...could she?

The real estate agent had kept her promise to turn the heat up. The furnishings had been moved out, the rooms echoing with emptiness and possibility. Clea wandered from one to the next, gazing out the windows at the stunning views of the bay and the offshore islands. She said dreamily, "We'd need a big oak dining room table and lots of carpets in rich colors—oh, Slade, look at the staircase!"

A gracious curve of highly polished walnut wound its way to the second floor. Like a woman enraptured, Clea climbed the stairs, her fingers caressing the railing. Slade followed, his attention more on Clea than on the details of the house. She liked it, he thought, his heart hammering in his chest. More than liked it.

The master bedroom faced the ocean. A stone fireplace was nestled between built-in bookshelves; the floor was pale birch. Clea went to stand by the window where she could gaze out at the gleaming blue water. How thoughtful of Slade, how loving of him, to find a house that reminded her of the one time in her childhood when she'd been truly happy.

He came up behind her. "It's a long way from civilization."

"If we kept our apartments in Manhattan and Milan, and your house in Florence," she said, "isolation would be nothing to worry about."

Our apartments, he thought giddily. "If there was a blizzard, we might be holed up for days."

"As long as we have a bed, that's fine with me."

"So buying a bed takes precedence over a fridge and stove?"

She turned to face him. Her sweater was tawny orange, her coat and slim wool slacks dark olive-green; once again, she was wearing the gold earrings he'd given her. Looping her arms around his neck, her eyes smiling into his, she said, "Are you suggesting I've got my priorities wrong?"

"I think you've got them exactly right," he said thickly, and kissed her at some length.

"I wish we did have a bed," she said, her voice muffled by his Aran-knit sweater.

He wanted, suddenly and desperately, to make love to her in this sun-drenched bedroom. "We could spread our coats on the floor, and there are a couple of blankets in the trunk of the car. For emergencies."

"This is an emergency. Why don't you go and get them?" she said, a gleam of pure mischief in her eye.

Slade took the stairs two at a time. He wanted to sing the Hallelujah Chorus. He wanted to waltz the length of the living room with Clea in his arms. He wanted to marry her.

One thing at a time, Slade. Blankets first. Marriage later.

When he went back upstairs, he stopped dead in the bedroom doorway. Clea was lying on the floor on top of her olive-green coat, wearing nothing but a smile and a pair of gold earrings. The light angled across her flank onto the smooth, pale birch.

Leaning against the door frame, the blankets draped over his arm, Slade started to laugh. "You have this unique capacity for taking me by surprise," he said. "But I bet you'd like a bit more padding between you and the floor."

"We're not using the missionary position—you're the one who's going to be underneath."

"Who says it's easy being a man?"

"Take off your clothes, Slade."

"Bossy, aren't you?" he replied, pulling his sweater over his head and starting to unbutton his shirt. "Imagine what we'll learn about each other should we live together." His fingers stilled. "Will you live with me, Clea?"

Sitting up in an entrancing flurry of bare limbs, she said, "I—I think so. I really am thinking hard about it." Then she frowned at her choice of words. "Not just thinking, that sounds too cold-blooded. I'm trying to feel what it would be like."

He asked the obvious. "How does it feel?"

"Terrifying—like I might fall off a cliff into the sea. Exciting—sharing a bed with you, joining our lives, traveling together." She tilted her head to one side. "We'd take turns putting out the garbage, right?"

"Absolutely."

"Oh God, Slade, I don't know. What if it didn't work out?"

"What if a comet collides with the earth?"

"Hmm...how long before you have to decide about the house?"

"I've got first refusal. It's not in my own best interests to rush you, Clea—I could buy the house anyway, and we'll wait and see." Every nerve in his body cried out against such a course; he wanted a decision from her now.

"I'm getting cold," she said. "Come and warm me, Slade."

Slade tossed her his shirt, warm from his body, and kicked the blankets over her way. "Don't forget how much I love you."

"I'm starting to trust that, too," she said in a low voice.

They made love slowly, almost in silence, as if it were a dream they were sharing: an intimacy all the more profound for its dependence on touch, on skin against skin rather than words. Afterward, rather than lingering on a floor that was rock-hard even with her coat and the two blankets underneath them, they got dressed and trailed downstairs through the empty rooms to the back door. Clea said softly, "I hate to leave."

"No one else will buy the house, I'll make sure of that."

She was holding his hand so tightly her knuckles were white. "We're going our separate ways tomorrow. You to Mexico City, me to Marseilles to see if a school there needs an addition."

"I'm back in two days and you're only gone for five."

She suddenly shivered, her features taut with distress. "I'm being silly. Let's go."

He ached to protect her, even to tell her to skip Marseilles and he'd deputize Mexico City. But that way, he knew, would lead to disaster: they both needed their independence. "I'm not going to disappear, Clea," he said forcefully. "I'm not going to let you down. Nor will I vanish when the going gets tough—which it's bound to, sooner or later."

"You sound so serious."

"Not all the vows are found in the marriage service."

She gave herself a little shake, doing her best to banish her unease. "Let's go back to the inn and try their fish chowder. New England in a bowl, isn't that what you called it?"

They got in the car and drove away from the house without a backward look.

Slade returned from Mexico three days before Clea was due back from Marseilles. Too restless to simply wait for her, he flew north to Maine the next day. After spending a couple of hours with a crusty old man who was researching wind power, Slade drove to the house. He was going to buy it right away, rather than wait for Clea's decision.

She loved the house. That was the clincher.

He went through the rooms one by one, taking note of needed repairs; in the bedroom, he stood in the doorway smiling foolishly at the smooth birch floor. Then he checked the spacious garage and the other outbuildings. Finally, tucking his trousers into his high boots, he started tramping through the woods behind the garage.

The real estate agent had mentioned that the original house, built by the first owners of the land well over a hundred years ago, was still standing. "You'd want to demolish it," the woman had said. "Hazardous in the extreme—I'm surprised the present owners didn't have it taken down."

The sun was sinking toward some low clouds, the temperature dropping. He'd give himself another ten minutes, then he'd head back to the car and civilization.

He'd be seeing Clea very soon. Had a man ever fallen in love so thoroughly, so inescapably, as he had outside the nightclub in Ardlaufen?

Through the gloomy trees, Slade saw the dark bulk of walls and a roof. Stepping carefully between the jagged-limbed spruce, he approached the old house. The roofline sagged. The windows were black holes, the front door hanging on its hinges.

A frisson traveled his spine. A family had lived here once, raised children, gone out in boats upon the sea. What was left to show of their lives but a tumbledown house, its dreams abandoned to the encroaching forest?

He almost turned back, wanting lights and warmth. Wanting to talk to Clea, and reassure himself that she was real.

Chiding himself for being overly imaginative, Slade pushed the door open. The hinges squealed like an animal in a trap. But the floorboards, he noticed, were foot-wide softwood, a few of them still with vestiges of polish. Others, though, were clearly rotten, where the roof had leaked.

He stepped inside, treading gingerly, keeping to the edges of the floor. In the parlor he found some old photos on the wall; as he reached for one of them to see if anything was written on the back, a signal shrilled from his jacket pocket, making him jump.

His cell phone. Symbol of the twenty-first century.

He took it out of his pocket and flipped it open. "Carruthers," he said.

"Slade? It's Clea. Slade, are you there?"

"Yeah, I'm here." He gripped the phone, the distress in her voice going right through him. "What's wrong? Where are you?"

"I'm at Lexington airport. I got a call from Byron—my mother's husband. Mother's had a heart attack. Byron says it's not serious, but I don't trust him—so I flew back from Marseilles early." She hesitated, then took the plunge. "Slade, could you come right away? I thought I could handle this on my own. But I can't. I—I need you. I need you to be with me."

"Sure I'll come," he said instantly. Clea, admitting that she needed him? He'd move heaven and earth to get to her side.

"You will?"

"Of course—isn't that what this is all about? I'll be there as soon as I can—I'm in Maine, at the house. Why don't I call you when I get to Newark? That way you'll know when to expect me."

"Thank you," she said, overwhelmed with relief. "How inadequate that sounds—but I really mean it."

"I'll be there sometime tonight, I promise. Hang in, sweetheart. Byron may well be telling the truth."

"You're right, he could be. I'm sorry, I'm so upset I can't think straight. I'd better go—I'm taking a cab to the hospital and I'll probably stay there all night. But I'll see you later on."

"I love you," Slade said forcefully. "Don't ever forget that. I hope your mother will be all right, and I'll see you as soon as possible—I can stay at the hospital with you. Bye for now." Still clutching his cell phone, his mind totally focused on Clea, alone in an airport in Kentucky, Slade rushed out of the parlor and across the kitchen floor.

With the soft, doughy sound of rotten wood, a whole section of the floorboards gave way. Thrown sideways, he made a frantic grab for the edge of the boards. His cell phone inscribed a graceful arc in the air, landing with a small thunk near the bottom of the stairs.

The boards crumbled in his fingers.

His arms flung wide in a desperate attempt to find purchase, Slade plunged through the hole into the darkness of the
old cellar. His head cracked against a rock, one arm doubled
under him. For a split second his whole body was enveloped
in a burst of jagged light and in pain beyond belief.

Then, mercifully, darkness encompassed him.

CHAPTER THIRTEEN

HE WAS eleven years old. Alone, in the dark. Not knowing where he was, or why. Knowing nothing but an atavistic terror of the night.

His eyes were closed, Slade realized in a surge of relief. That was why it was dark. Slowly he opened them. Blackness pressed down on him, surrounding him with a dead, suffocating and impenetrable silence.

But he wasn't lying on the floorboards of the underground cupboard, whose pattern of cracks he'd memorized because there was nothing else to do. He was lying on rock. Hard. Cold. Damp, even through his clothes. Where was he?

His head hurt.

As he tried to shift position, a hoarse cry of agony burst from his lips. His arm was on fire, the bone lanced with a pain that made the darkness swoop and whirl. He lay very still.

As though ice water had been thrown in his face, Slade remembered where he was: in the cellar of the old house on the property in Maine. He'd fallen through the floor.

Clea. He'd been on his way to see Clea. Because she needed him.

With his good arm, he fumbled in his pocket for his cell phone, and then recalled with a wave of horror how it had flown from his hand to land at the foot of the stairs.

It might as well have landed on the moon.

Think, Slade. Think.

He had a pounding headache. When he lifted his fingers to his forehead, they came away sticky. He'd hit his head on the rock, that's what had happened. It had been dusk when he'd been exploring the old house. So he'd been unconscious; now it was night.

He wasn't a young boy locked in an airless cupboard. He was a grown man who couldn't afford to panic.

Then his memory supplied the last, devastating piece of the puzzle. Clea was spending the night in Kentucky with her mother. She must be wondering where he was, for she would have expected him to have arrived by now.

He'd promised to phone her from Newark.

From her perspective, he'd failed her, running away when the chips were down. Just like her father. Just like her mother whenever there was the slightest problem with any of her husbands.

He had to get out of here. Phone Clea and explain why he was in Maine and not in Kentucky.

In a single swift movement Slade rolled over. Pain engulfed him; his groan sounded like that of a wounded animal.

He bit his lip so hard he could taste blood, and looked at his watch face. Glowing in the dark, the numbers said 06:50. Ten to seven in the morning, he thought sickly. He'd been unconscious for over twelve hours.

Clea had spent the night at her mother's bedside alone.

He pushed himself upright on his good arm, the other one hanging limp at his side. Then, gritting his teeth, he got to his feet and staggered across the uneven floor, one hand held out in front of him so he wouldn't walk face-first into the wall. When his fingers brushed cold stone, he followed the wall along its length to the corner.

What felt like an age later, Slade arrived back where he'd begun. There was no door leading to the outside. But while he'd been searching for it, he'd stumbled over several loose rocks, some of them flat. He'd pile them up and climb out of the cellar that way.

Say it fast. Nothing to it.

His knees weak as a kitten's, Slade sank down onto the nearest rock and fashioned his belt into a sling for his broken arm. Afterward, he sat very still for a while, struggling to recover his strength.

Then his heart leaped in his chest. Was that light seeping through the floorboards? So that he could, for the first time, actually see the hole in the floor?

The very faintest of gray light—but it was still light. Hugely encouraged, his claustrophobia dissolving, Slade pushed himself upright again, and headed for the wall where he'd stubbed his toe against the largest of the loose rocks.

The rock was far too large to lift one-handed. Using his feet and one arm, he moved it, inch by slow inch, underneath the hole. And this rock, he thought grimly, was the easy one. The next one would have to be lifted on top of it.

The hole looked an enormous distance above his head.

Clea. Remember Clea.

Three hours later, grunting with effort, Slade got a fourth rock on the pile. Two more and he'd be home free.

Despite the cold, Slade was sweating copiously. He'd give his eyeteeth for a bottle of cold spring water. And a doughnut, he thought. Covered in maple cream and laden with trans fat.

Whipping cream, champagne and Clea…how he loved her. And how terrified he was that she'd fly straight from her mother's bedside to Europe, where she'd go into hiding, convinced that he'd betrayed her newfound trust.

How could he blame her for coming to that conclusion?

With renewed energy he got the fifth rock on the pile. Although the last rock was the hardest, eventually he got it in place, then spent half an hour jamming smaller stones into the gaps to stabilize the pile.

Afterward, Slade never wanted to remember how he got out of the cellar. He did know it took every last ounce of his strength and determination. He simply couldn't afford to be defeated. Too much was at stake.

The hardest part was finding an edge of the floor to cling to that wasn't rotten, meanwhile teetering on the pile of rocks. With a final shove, using all the power of his leg muscles, he thrust himself onto the floorboards and rolled onto his side, panting, his eyes closed. He'd never again dismiss a broken arm as a trivial injury.

His cell phone was at the foot of the stairs.

Craning his neck, he looked at his watch. One o'clock, he thought through the red mist in his head. Clea could be in mid-Atlantic by now. Winging her way east.

He pushed himself to his knees and, inch by inch, distributing his weight as evenly as he could, crawled toward the stairs and his cell phone.

"Slade! Are you inside? Slade, where are you?"

He was hallucinating. He had to be, if he was hearing Clea's voice when she was hundreds of miles away. Digging his nails into the old plaster of the wall, Slade hauled himself to his feet.

A shadow fell across his body. He looked over his shoulder.

Clea was standing in the open doorway. As she stepped over the threshold, he gasped, "Stop! The floor's rotten."

Her dazed eyes went from the gaping hole in the floorboards back to him. "Your head," she said in a voice he scarcely recognized. "It's bleeding. And your arm—"

"I fell into the cellar," he said, suddenly acutely uncomfortable. "It's taken me all this time to get out."

"Slade, you could have been killed…"

"No more than I deserved—it was a damn fool thing to do."

She made a tiny gesture with her hands, unable to bear feeling so useless. "I'm coming to help you—you look like you're going to fall flat on your face."

"Stay put, Clea. That's an order."

He edged toward her, keeping as close as he could to the walls with their peeling wallpaper. Finally he reached the doorway, standing only inches from her. She was wearing a blue parka and jeans, her eyes huge, her face pale. "I've been out of my mind with worry," she faltered, and burrowed her face into his shoulder, needing to know he was real. Safe in her arms.

Keeping his broken arm out of the way, he pulled her toward him, resting his cheek on her hair. "I'm so sorry, Clea," he muttered. "I figured you'd head straight back to Europe and I'd never see you again."

"I thought of it, believe me."

"Why didn't you?"

"I'm here, that's what counts," she said. "My car's parked by the house—luckily you left the gates unlocked. I'm taking you to the nearest hospital and we'll talk after that."

"I don't suppose you have any coffee with you? Or even water?"

"Hot coffee and blueberry muffins, in the car."

"You're nominated for sainthood."

"Some of my thoughts the last twenty-four hours have been far from saintly. Put your good arm over my shoulder."

"I can manage on my—"

"Do as you're told," Clea flared, wondering how she could be angry when he'd just scared her out of ten years' growth.

"Okay. Only because I'm not sure my legs can hold me up. Do you promise to turn the heater on full blast?"

"I do. Let's go."

"Like I said, bossy." But as he looped his arm over her shoulder, he added huskily, "Thanks, Clea. For hanging in."

Her vision wavered. "You're welcome."

The ground was uneven, and the trees too close for comfort. But eventually they reached Clea's rented car. "We'll leave your car here and send someone for it," she said. "Give me the keys and I'll lock the gates on our way out."

"My overnight bag's in my car, could you get it?" He passed over the keys and sank down into the passenger seat. His heart was thudding and his hairline wet with sweat. Clea shut his door, walked around the hood and got in beside him.

She reached down by his feet, picking up a thermos and pouring him a mug of steaming coffee, glad to have something concrete to do. The alternative was to break down and weep like a baby, which wouldn't be the slightest bit helpful.

"This coffee's divine," Slade mumbled. "You did say muffin, didn't you?"

As he devoured the muffin, Clea circled the driveway, stopping beyond the gates. After she'd locked them behind her, she took a blanket from the backseat and bundled it to support his sling. "Is your arm broken, do you think?"

"Gotta be—hurts like hell."

"We'll be at the hospital in half an hour," she said, turning onto the highway.

He had to get it over with. "I was rushing across the kitchen right after getting your phone call, not watching what I was doing, and the boards gave way. Cracked myself on the head on the rock in the cellar and was out like a light for over twelve hours."

"In an underground place in the dark...no wonder you look so awful. You shouldn't be talking, Slade—just rest."

"I need to talk...I couldn't bear to think about you waiting for me to arrive, waiting and waiting, then gradually realizing I wasn't going to come just when you needed me. That I'd failed you. Betrayed you in the cruelest way possible."

She said steadily, "I did feel all those things. It was a very long night, and I hope I never again feel as low as I did at four a.m. The only bright spot was that my mother was much better than I'd anticipated, so at least I didn't have to worry about her. Although I did make the mistake of telling her you were flying down to be with me."

Slade's very pungent swearword brought a smile to Clea's lips. "You said it. Early this morning when it was all too clear you hadn't turned up or sent a message, and that you weren't even answering your cell phone, Mother started to rub it in. Men, she said, bastards all of them, their promises as useless as—er, certain other parts of their anatomy. None of them can be trusted, and the rich ones are the worst…you get the picture. At first I went along with it because it really had been a dreadful night—every time I heard footsteps in the corridor, I thought it was you."

"And it never was," Slade supplied grimly.

"But around the time the sun came up, I told Mother to keep her opinions to herself, and I started to think. About you. How you said you'd never let me down because you were different from my father and all my mother's husbands. That's when I decided something must have gone wrong. Then Bill—with whom I'm on speaking terms again—told me you hadn't come back from Maine. I got on a flight north by the skin of my teeth, and drove straight to the house."

"You trusted me," Slade said dazedly.

"Once I stopped paying attention to Mother, I did." Clea hesitated, her eyes on the winding road. "I still do. And I was right to, wasn't I?"

"I can't tell you how I regret putting you through all that."

"Nothing like listening to my mother on the subject of men for bringing me to my senses." She glanced sideways at him. "There's something I really regret, too—I ought to have called the police before I flew up here. You'd have been rescued so much sooner."

"I'm glad you didn't," Slade said emphatically. "Sirens. Ambulances. Reports to file. Omigod."

"We both did okay, then," she said contentedly.

"You did superlatively, Clea. Splendiferously."

Her smile felt as wide as her face. "To have finally realized that I can trust you—what an amazing feeling."

"Worth falling into several cellars."

"Will you be able to make love with your arm in a cast?" she said pertly.

"Trust me," he said.

"I will," she chuckled. "After all, I've got to keep in practice…we should be nearly there."

Within five minutes Clea was parking near the emergency entrance of the local hospital. As they walked toward the glass doors, Slade caught sight of his own reflection: unshaven, dried blood encrusted in his hair and down his face, his skin and clothes filthy. "Is that me?" he gasped.

"They wouldn't hire you for the cover of *Gentleman's Quarterly.*"

"An ad for detergent, more like."

"The heavy-duty kind," she said, holding the door open. The inevitable forms had to be filled in, they waited for the appropriate doctor, then for X-rays, and finally the cast was applied. By the time they left the hospital, Slade was too tired even to be hungry.

Clea said easily, "I booked a room in a country inn down the road. They'll have dinner ready for us. The nurse said you can have a shower as long as you keep the cast dry."

The medication he'd been given for his headache was making him drowsy; it seemed a very long time since he'd last slept. The inn, decorated in a romantic extravaganza of roses, was a blur to him. He showered and dressed with difficulty, ate what was put in front of him and climbed the stairs again with Clea at his side.

The wide bed, canopied and with a rose-strewn duvet, looked as near to heaven as he could imagine. Clea helped him undress. Wearing only his briefs, he lay down. "Come here," he muttered, "I want to hold on to you." And fell asleep.

When Slade woke, the first thing he saw was a pretty flowered lamp shade, its bulb a soft glow in the darkness, sitting on a table with a long flowered skirt.

Clea was curled into his chest, her breathing the deep, even rhythm of sleep. Her hair was a tangled, fiery mass of curls on the pillow. The pillow slip was embroidered with roses.

Such an uprush of love filled his body that he could scarcely contain it. She hadn't run off to Europe without him. She'd come looking for him instead.

How did he ever get to be so lucky?

She must have left the lamp on so he wouldn't, even for a moment, think he was still trapped in a dark cellar.

With his good hand, he stroked the hair back from her face, then kissed her cheek, letting his mouth slide down the slender column of her throat. Her eyes flickered open. "Slade?" she murmured.

"Hello, my darling."

As she stretched lazily against him, her eyes widened. "Well," she said, "you're recovering just fine."

"Do you think we should find out if I can make love with a broken arm?"

"Nothing like the present," she said, wriggling to face him and running her fingers up his bare chest.

He said huskily, "Everything I've ever wanted is here in my arms," and bent his head to kiss her.

They made love with a quiet intensity, broken only by little bursts of laughter as the cast inevitably got in the way. When he slid within her, knowing he'd come home, he could feel her trembling and throbbing with need in every nerve he possessed. As climax shuddered through her, he rose to meet her, emptying himself even as he was suffused with a love so strong, so overwhelming, that he could scarcely breathe. Their hearts, he thought dimly, were hammering as one, even as their bodies were one.

In the lamplight Clea smiled at him. How could there be a better time than this, she thought, and said, "I have something to tell you."

"You're flying back to Marseilles first thing in the morning."

"And leaving you here? No way."

"You're going to wear a red leather miniskirt to Belle's next garden party."

Chuckling, Clea pressed her fingers to his lips. "Be quiet and listen. Slade, do you know what's happened? It's so wonderful—I've fallen in love with you."

He lay very still. He was dreaming. He must be. "Say that again."

Shyly she looked up at him, her lips swollen from his kisses, her cheeks a warm pink. "You heard me—I love you."

"I've wondered if I'd ever hear you say that. Oh, sweetheart, I love you, too."

He held her close, filled with a happiness as deep as the ocean, as sure as the tides. She said, easing herself into the circle of his arm, "Now that I look back, I guess I fell in love with you in Chamonix. But I was into denial in a big way. Me, in love? Absolutely not."

"I noticed," Slade said dryly.

"It wasn't until I was waiting for you, hour after hour, at my mother's bedside, that I realized the truth." She gave a reminiscent shudder at the memory of that excruciating vigil. "Terrible timing. I'd finally fallen in love, but with a man who'd abandoned me just when I needed him. I told you it was a long night. And then when I figured something must have happened to you—that was even worse."

"Marry me, Clea."

"Yes," she said.

"Just like that? You're sure?"

"I love you, I'll marry you and live by your side, we'll have children, we'll invite your parents for lunch on Sundays and I'll learn how to make smoked salmon fish cakes."

"Nothing half-hearted about you, my darling."

"I can't tell you how happy I feel! I love you, Slade. And I love telling you that I love you."

As he laughed deep in his chest, his arms hard around her, she added, "Maybe, once in a while, we'll even invite my mother for lunch. Because you're right, Slade, underneath it all she's scared silly."

He smiled at her, his heart in his eyes. "We can invite Lothar, if you like. And Bill—you and he are practically old friends."

She gave a contented sigh. "No more meeting in bars."

"No more costume museums."

"No more strobe lights. Are we going to turn into a deadly boring couple sitting by the fireside night after night?"

"I can't imagine life with you being the slightest bit boring," Slade said. "In bed or out."

"Let's phone your parents and invite them to the wedding."

"Later," he said firmly. "For now, just in case you're worried about boredom creeping up on us, I think we should stay exactly where we are."

Clea ran her fingers suggestively down his body. "The dining room doesn't open for another two hours."

"Good," said Slade.

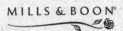

FREE!

4 Books
and a surprise gift!

We would like to take this opportunity to thank you for reading this Mills & Boon® book by offering you the chance to take FOUR more specially selected titles from the Modern Romance™ series absolutely FREE! We're also making this offer to introduce you to the benefits of the Reader Service™—

- ★ FREE home delivery
- ★ FREE gifts and competitions
- ★ FREE monthly Newsletter
- ★ Exclusive Reader Service offers
- ★ Books available before they're in the shops

Accepting these FREE books and gift places you under no obligation to buy, you may cancel at any time, even after receiving your free shipment. Simply complete your details below and return the entire page to the address below. You don't even need a stamp!

YES! Please send me 4 free Modern Romance books and a surprise gift. I understand that unless you hear from me, I will receive 6 superb new titles every month for just £2.80 each, postage and packing free. I am under no obligation to purchase any books and may cancel my subscription at any time. The free books and gift will be mine to keep in any case.

P6ZEF

Ms/Mrs/Miss/Mr .... Initials ....

Surname .... **BLOCK CAPITALS PLEASE**

Address ....

....

.... Postcode ....

Send this whole page to:
UK: FREEPOST CN81, Croydon, CR9 3WZ